This is like Kafka in Deoria. Or Camus in the cow belt. But more accurate to say that *Legal Fiction* is an urgent, literary report about how truth goes missing in our land. I read it with a racing heart.

— AMITAVA KUMAR, author of *The Lovers*

Chandan Pandey goes looking for the story that lurks just out of sight, getting under the skin of news headlines and extracting a story that is as compelling as it is devastating.

— ANNIE ZAIDI, author of *Prelude to a Riot*

Chandan Pandey has written a brilliant, gripping political novel. *Legal Fiction* is a nuanced, absorbing snapshot of our times — it captures the minefield of hate politics, the intricate, almost invisible fault lines in relationships, and the power of art in imagining a better society.

— MEENA KANDASAMY, author of *When I Hit You*

The Hindi novel was already destined to be a marker for this era. Now this translation fills a big gap, for no work originally written in English in India has scratched the surface of what *Legal Fiction* approaches the cold, dark centre of. Here, in the form of a thriller and the tone of an elegy, is a sharp look at a terrifying Indian *-ism* and the currents against it. Be ready for a heart of darkness.

— TANUJ SOLANKI, author of *Diwali in Muzaffarnagar*

LEGAL FICTION

A Novel

CHANDAN PANDEY

TRANSLATED BY
BHARATBHOOSHAN TIWARI

HARPER**PERENNIAL**

An Imprint of HarperCollins Publishers

First published in English in India in 2021 by Harper Perennial
An imprint of HarperCollins *Publishers*
A-75, Sector 57, Noida, Uttar Pradesh 201301, India
www.harpercollins.co.in

2 4 6 8 10 9 7 5 3 1

Originally published in Hindi as
Vaidhanik Galp © Chandan Pandey 2020
English translation © Bharatbhooshan Tiwari 2021

P-ISBN: 978-93-5422-750-9
E-ISBN: 978-93-5422-446-1

Typeset in 11/15.2 Warnock Pro at
Manipal Technologies Limited, Manipal

Printed and bound at
Thomson Press (India) Ltd

MIX
Paper
FSC® C010615

This book is produced from independently certified FSC® paper
to ensure responsible forest management.

For Shruti

Everything in *Legal Fiction* is fiction. All that is fiction is fiction, of course, but even the truth is fiction. If the people, stories, places and incidents at any point appear to be true, it is our collective misfortune. We advise you to consider it a fault of the imagination and move on.

The chariot of time lies besieged somewhere – a line from Shamsher Bahadur Singh's poem comes to me, not as a reference but as a forgotten friend.

(27/8/15, from Rafique's diary)

DAY ONE

DAY ONE

It MUST HAVE BEEN SOMETIME around eleven at night when my phone rang, and Mohammad Rafi's pitch-perfect voice called out: *'Mujhe apni sharan mein le lo Ram...'* The phone was with Archana. I was at my writing desk at home, going through a book that had been lost for several years among my bookshelves. I was often reminded of the book, and after suddenly finding it today, I tried to understand why I had made so many marks and underlined the text in several places. The underlined passages were still fascinating, but why had I marked them up? What had been on my mind when I did that? I had even put down a few exclamation points, but I couldn't remember why. So, I wanted to read the book all over again, taking notes this time, in order to imbibe the text fully.

When Archana entered the office and stood between the desk and the light, I realized she had brought the mobile phone with her. She handed it to me.

'Is that Arjun Kumar speaking?'

The voice had a Haryanvi brusqueness. I sensed an anxiety in its tone, as if it urgently wanted to tell me something.

'Yes. And you?'

Archana was standing in front of me. The voice rang out in the quiet of the night. It was a woman, and Archana could also hear her.

'This is Anasuya,' the woman said.

'Anasuya who?' I asked, but I immediately remembered who she was. 'Oh!' I blurted out. Archana looked at the whirling emotions on my face. 'You!' Then, after a pause, I said, 'Long time...'

I could sense she was relieved that I had not forgotten her. Perhaps that was why she got rid of the honorary 'aap' in the very next sentence and became more informal. 'You are Arjun Kumar the writer, yes?'

'Yes, if people consider me to be one.' I had no idea whether I said this for Anasuya's benefit, or for Archana's, or for a world that had an unwarranted hold over language. Anyway, that was a larger question. At that moment, however, I couldn't understand why she had called, and that too, so late at night.

'I read a short story of yours in a newspaper, perhaps in *Dainik Jagriti*, many years ago.'

'That was around five years ago.' I grew worried about the impression she would have formed of me had she read only that one story. When she became silent, I felt she might be crying. Archana continued to stand right there, looking at the bookshelf.

'Arjun, my husband has not returned home since yesterday morning.'

Dear reader, I should tell you that I have completed her sentence here, for she had begun to sob almost as soon as she started to speak. Hearing her sobs, Archana gestured at me to turn on the speaker phone.

'What are you saying?' I asked but got annoyed at my ridiculous question. She was simply telling me about her situation.

'I have been to the police station twice today. But no one's telling me anything.' She paused as her voice choked up with emotion. I heard her take a deep breath before she resumed, 'Three policemen just came home. The landlord literally begged them to go away. They've searched the entire house twice already.'

'Where are you?'

Such a strange question. Someone you'd spent a long period of your life with – after a while, you don't even know whether they exist or not.

'Noma,' she said. Then, thinking I wouldn't know where Noma was, she added, 'Salempur', then 'Deoria'. Perhaps she still wasn't satisfied, so she finally said, 'It's near Gorakhpur.'

'He will come back. Why don't you go to a friend's place and wait until tomorrow morning?' I wanted to ask if her husband was an addict, but I couldn't muster the courage. Such questions cut deep – even if he wasn't an addict, it would have hit her hard.

'Nobody from the police is listening to me.' She began to wail. The room reverberated with the sound. They were the sort of cries that could make you forget who you were.

'Wait until the morning,' I repeated.

'You don't understand, Arjun. I'm in big trouble. I don't know anyone with connections in the police force. They're not even filing a missing-person report—' And the call got disconnected.

Only after the call got disconnected did it strike me that I rarely came across statements such as 'You don't understand' or 'Try to understand'. I usually went silent after such declarations and no longer had the drive to continue with the conversation.

Something was going on in Archana's mind. We stayed quiet, and silence took over the room. The silence persisted, but now we were mutely staring at each other. Then I asked, 'What do you think?' It was my attempt to break the silence. I didn't really want to know what she thought, but immediately Archana said, 'You must go.' Then she added, 'I will speak to my brother too.'

A person has to be insane to not get worried when someone they love doesn't come home, or to not be baffled when their husband suddenly disappears. Anasuya's troubles were becoming clearer just as the darkness was beginning to lift outside. And we'd been more than just acquaintances. I was worried about her, but it had never occurred to me to go out of my way to help anyone, and it didn't sit well with me now. I couldn't even remember the last time I had spent my time and energy to help someone. Any assistance that I offered had been, at best, restricted to giving away some money.

Archana held up the phone. The MakeMyTrip app was open. I could see an Air India flight listed on it. 'It takes off at 5.15 a.m. and lands in Gorakhpur an hour and a half later,' she said.

Saying so, she turned to leave. I didn't want to go. Even if I did, I would rather take a train. But as she walked away, Archana seemed to sense my thoughts and said decisively, 'All trains depart later in the day and it's impossible to get a ticket now.'

There were a couple of reasons why I didn't want to go.

First, I knew where Noma was. And second, Archana and I had quarrelled over this very Anasuya a few years ago. That squabble had dragged on for almost a fortnight, and the word 'divorce' had come up for the first time between us. In the days that followed, I caught myself more than once wondering whether it was truly possible for the two of us to be divorced.

The quarrel had started with a bookshelf. I don't remember now whether we had been fighting about where to place it or how to arrange books in it. But during our argument, an old photograph fell out of my copy of *Ashvamedha Yagna*. The photograph was several years old. A girl wearing a blue-and-white college uniform pretended as if she were flying. All her weight was on her left leg, her right leg was raised behind her and bent at the knee. Her lips were pouted as if for a kiss. A boy stood beside her, laughing. Both looked into the camera.

'Who is this?' Archana had asked me.

'Me.'

'I can see that. But who is this girl by your side?'

I could not recall her name at that moment. The argument got much worse before a truce was finally called. Then, some ten or twelve days later, while we sat drinking tea in the evening, her name came to me, and I simply uttered it aloud: 'Anasuya.' Although there would be more occasions when names of other girls would come up between us, the fallout of that argument was such that Anasuya was never mentioned again.

Whatever the true reasons for Archana's anger may have been then, the apparent one was that I had never told her about Anasuya. I wasn't prepared for her onslaught. Holding on to old photographs and letters is a strange disease, I admit, but it is one that I am afflicted by. And what was the big deal about an old photo anyway? If I had wanted to tip-toe around this fact, I could have simply told Archana the name of an old friend she knew about.

Before I could pursue this train of thought further, Archana said, 'Call Anasuya immediately, tell her you're coming. She must be getting worried.' After a pause, she calmly added, 'If you don't mind, can I speak to her?'

I realized that Archana must be thinking along entirely different lines. She must be thinking that I wanted to stay away from Anasuya because of our past. But the truth was that I did not want to go to Noma. It's preposterous to call someone after years and expect them to turn up immediately. And Archana knew I did not like to travel at all.

I knew about Deoria very well. A certain 'Deoraha Baba' had influenced my father quite a bit, and he said Deoria had got its name because of the godman. There was another recent bit of news about how a policeman had saved a couple from a mob in a town called Deoria. But above all, I had been writing a story on Anjan Agarwal, an MLA from Deoria. He had won the elections despite being on the run. I had always been fascinated by the nexus between the police and politicians. In this case, the helplessness of the police was most interesting; they could not arrest Agarwal even when the nefarious criminal was filing his nomination papers for the elections. If I had to go to Noma, I would try and meet the legislator or his supporters.

While Archana booked the ticket, I searched online for news from Deoria, Noma and Gorakhpur. Most were related to the legislator or his businesses. A couple of news items from Noma spoke about a 'deemed' university and sounded like advertorials pretending to be news. One spoke about a Union minister's impending visit to the town to inaugurate the famous fair of Dol Mela. This news item was full of pictures. I kept going through the sites of various newspapers. But there was nothing about a missing person. Then I realized I should have asked Anasuya her husband's name.

In my rush to catch the flight and with all the anxiety on my mind, I made a mistake.

It's difficult to reach the Delhi airport from Gurgaon in the early hours of the morning – the state road tax is so high that Ola and Uber cabs do not want to cross the border. Sometimes, they cancel on their own. You are then left to fend for yourself, the imminent risk of missing your flight notwithstanding.

This is exactly what happened. Anything that had to go wrong, did – Murphy's Law in action. Two cabs cancelled on me, and I did not know what to do.

Hurriedly, Archana decided to drop me at the airport. Except for a passing remark about Archana calling her older brother Ravi later in the day, we spent the half-hour ride in silence.

Ravi Bhaiyya was a sore point with me. He was in a powerful position in the Ministry of Home Affairs. We had come to loggerheads over trivial issues several times in the past. He did not like me and had no qualms about making it known every now and then. Although the feeling was reciprocated, my failures had put me in a position where I could not criticize him openly, especially since he had done us a lot of favours. Although Archana got her job on her own merit, my job had come about as a result of his recommendation. Around seven or eight years ago, when Archana and I were newlyweds, Ravi Bhaiyya would say he liked my poems, and that since his sister had chosen me, there had to be something in me. But as the years passed, I fell behind.

At the airport, when Archana repeated that she would call Ravi Bhaiyya, I realized that she had been asking for my opinion the first time, but now she was simply informing me. 'Fly back this evening or tomorrow morning. If Anasuya is in trouble, bring her with you. Whatever the situation is, let me know and I will book the tickets accordingly,' she said.

If it wasn't for the lines we drew around ourselves outside of darkened rooms, I would have embraced her right there, outside the airport. But those lines found us a rationale for not doing so – there was no parking space, and she would be fined if she got down from the vehicle.

In any case, by the time I emerged from the slumber of my thoughts, the car had begun to pull away.

The fact that I did not hug my wife goodbye was not the mistake I was talking about. Rather, I asked Anasuya her husband's name over SMS, texting her while boarding the aircraft: 'What was your husband's name?'

A thought sprung out of nowhere, either because of the message I'd sent Anasuya or because of the relief I felt upon reaching the airport on time. I wanted to see if I knew someone in Gorakhpur, Deoria, Salempur or Noma. I thought of saying something on my Facebook or Twitter, but then, language presented itself as an obstacle.

Language and vocabulary render us helpless in moments of despair – a helplessness one can only express in language. Words abandon us, and one doesn't know the right ones to use. What could I have written, then? That my ex's husband hadn't returned home for three days? Or that I had once abandoned an extraordinary woman, and now her husband had gone missing? What could I have written?

If Archana hadn't known anything, I could have lied. But it would be embarrassing to lie when she knew the truth. I ruminated on my words as my finger hovered over Noma on Google Maps. Then, paying no heed to what Archana might think, I finally wrote: 'A family friend of ours has not returned home for the past three days. He lives in Noma, close to Deoria or Gorakhpur. If there is someone on my list who lives close by, please contact me. I am on my way to Noma.'

I posted it on Facebook and Twitter, then went over it again and again. I read it from Archana's perspective. She would usually be on Facebook in the afternoons. Would she laugh while reading this, knowing what the truth was? What would she say? She'd make fun of me for calling a man whose name I didn't know a 'family friend'.

I realized my mistake just as the aircraft was about to take off.

Why had I asked Anasuya 'What *was* your husband's name?' The 'was' pierced right through me like a nail. If the soul could bleed, mine would be spewing fountains. I began to worry about Anasuya for the first time. Who was I to have asked her about her husband in the past tense? I shouldn't have written 'was'. My second mistake was that I made her aware of my first mistake – growing anxious, I shot off another message, simply typing '*is*'. But what did that even mean? That's when I committed my third mistake – I sent her yet another message: 'What is your husband's name?'

Before I could get a reply, the airhostess asked us to turn our phones off. I saw several passengers continue to click pictures of the sky outside, of themselves, or of those accompanying them. I saw an elderly woman loudly asking someone to come pick her up when she landed. I saw the airhostess then individually request each passenger to turn their phones off.

What I didn't see all this while was how Anasuya would read my three messages.

I turned my phone on as soon as we landed. Two messages popped up one after another:

'Bhaiyya will call you. He was mad at me. Keep me informed.'

'Rafique Neel.'

The taxi driver outside the airport slept with his legs on the steering wheel. He was wearing a blue kurta-pyjama. He looked like a short man, but when he stepped out, I could see he was at least six and a half feet tall.

'Will you go to Noma?' I asked him.

'Two thousand eight hundred.'

'Both ways.'

'Will we be stopping there?'

'At most until tomorrow maybe.'

He took a good look at me. 'Three thousand per day. And you will have to pay the toll.'

'As you wish.'

He introduced himself as Sahadeo and helped me load my luggage in the boot. Before turning on the engine, he did a pranam to the steering wheel. He kept the engine running for a little while and began skimming through a newspaper.

'You get *Dainik Jagriti* here as well?' I asked over the rumbling engine. He handed the paper to me without looking and started driving.

It's my habit to read the newspaper starting from the back pages. The front pages usually have the same old news about government matters. Except for the sports page, there was hardly any news you couldn't predict. This particular edition had no editorial. Instead, there was a page called 'Arogya Darshan' – philosophy of wellness. The fourth page was titled 'Deoria Jagriti' and had five sections. Under the 'In and around Rudrapur' section, there was a news item about a fire at a petrol pump that had been put out on time. Another section was titled 'In and around Barhaj'.

As I began reading, my phone rang: 'Ravi Bhaiyya calling'. I took the call and wished him, 'Hello Bhaiyya, pranam.' I heard him bless me. As he began saying something, my attention shifted to the two sections at the bottom of the page: 'In and around Tamkuhi' and 'In and around Salempur'.

Ravi Bhaiyya was bristling. He was asking me to take the next flight home.

'Sure,' I said noncommittally and continued reading the paper.

Under 'In and around Salempur', there were five reports. The one in the centre was accompanied by colour pictures. It was clearly the lead: 'Preparations on in Full Swing for Noma's Dol Mela'. The first picture showed an empty fairground; the second was captioned, 'Officers surveying mela preparations'. A photograph of the Mela Committee's chair S.P. Malviya (Dadda) had been placed within the news. Another advertisement, placed by some 'Mangal Morcha', welcomed a Union minister who was supposed to inaugurate the fair. Finally, there was a short news piece: 'Student Missing'. A girl's passport photo had been printed with it. The photograph was faded, but I could make out a wide forehead, a straight nose, and some sort of a birthmark below the eyes. I couldn't make out the girl's complexion, but even in this black-and-white image, I could see she was attractive.

> *Noma, 3 August. Janaki Dubey, a student at Swami Devanand Degree College, has been missing since the last two days. She had left home for college on Saturday. When she didn't return that evening, her father went to her college to check. There, the other students told him she had not come at all that day.*

Bhaiyya handed the phone over to his wife. She too had an entire list of instructions for me. Failure brings with it plenty of guardians. I put the phone on mute and kept it aside as my sister-in-law continued to speak. I asked Sahadeo, 'How far is Noma?'

'Pretty far,' he said, then added with a chuckle, 'Seventy kilometres.'

Soon, we entered a dense forest. I asked him to roll down the windows. There were teak trees all around us. The dark road ran between them. The sun hadn't climbed in the sky, so the trees threw long shadows on the road. We crossed one shadow after another quickly. Occasionally, I could see trails disappearing into the jungle. Did people live inside?

Sahadeo said, 'This is called the Kushmi jungle. Once, it spread as far as Assam, but no longer.'

I was familiar with this forest. But I had read that it had once stretched not till Assam but till Nepal.

HER CALLER TUNE WAS A pleasing flute melody. It continued to play, but my call went unanswered. I tried once more but didn't get a response. I paused to check whether I had dialled the correct number. I hadn't even been able to ask Archana about her conversation with Anasuya.

Anasuya called back. The Truecaller app showed her name as 'Anasuya Neel'.

The spontaneity of our previous night's conversation aside, I did not know how to talk to her. Ours was a broken relationship. When siblings or a couple quarrel and don't talk to each other for a few days, it's difficult to begin speaking again. Imagine my quandary, for Anasuya and my relationship had ended about a dozen years ago. But then, it wouldn't be appropriate for me to feel the same for her after so many years either.

'There's no news yet.'

'I will reach in a couple of hours.'

'If you know someone, please have them call the police. They haven't even filed an FIR.' She continued, 'A few of Rafique's students had come over. They were talking about going to the police station together.'

She seemed to be speaking to me from an entirely different universe. I had been thinking that Anasuya wouldn't even have realized she was calling her ex-boyfriend when she phoned me. She just needed help. If there was anyone else who could have helped her, she wouldn't have reached out to me. She would have called her friends first, and then perhaps with some hesitation, even her enemies. Only when there was no one else she could reach out to would she have thought of me. This was not a call from an old flame. When I learnt that she was married to a teacher, I felt glad for a moment. It meant that her life had been going well before this incident.

'Reach the police station by ten. I will see you all there,' I said emphatically. As a postscript, I added, 'Send me your location on Google Maps, if possible.'

I was reminded that the previous night, Archana had shared my Google Maps location with her Google account, and registered her own location on my phone. She had asked me not to turn off the internet. To me, this was all new – a tool with which one could instantly find out where the other person was.

Two triangles – in red and blue – were painted on the police station's door. They would have made a rectangle had they been the same colour. The police station itself was massive, perhaps the largest I had seen. The southern end of the town. A lawn spread out over three acres or more, and

a two-storeyed building right in the middle, haveli-like
and surrounded by a tall wall. It looked like it had been a
residence once, before being converted into a police station.

From here, the town looked as if it was far away, and
ugly. If one came from Gorakhpur to Noma via Deoria and
Salempur, the station appeared like a gateway to the town.
But it was, in fact, outside the town. From here, one could
see a stretch of buildings begin. A town settled in a long,
straight line – the way settlements built along riverbanks
usually are. Except, there was no river here, only a road that
cut through the town. If someone came here to have fun or
to visit, they would most certainly be disappointed.

Perhaps because the police station was outside the town,
tempos, vikrams and autorickshaws thronged near it. A
tea stall stood beneath a mahua tree. With overcast skies,
the weather was perfect for some tea, but none among the
twenty-odd people around the stall seemed to have such a
thought.

This was the first time in my life that I was at a police
station.

It would be incorrect to say I thought of Anasuya
immediately after stepping out of the car. She and the
trouble she found herself in were on my mind, but I wasn't
able to find any structure for my thoughts. Amidst the
jumble of incomplete thoughts, a face would sneak in every
now and then, and a name would flash: Anasuya. I kept
mouthing her name. Sahadeo had even asked me many
times during the ride, 'Did you say something?'

I wondered whether I would even be able to recognize her. A deep anxiety crouched at my mind's door like a terrified kitten.

The police station was crowded. Around fifty people seemed to be there, gathered in groups of four or five, standing almost equidistant from each other like trees in an orchard. Nobody spoke loudly, but everybody was saying something. So, the police station, or orchard if you will, was abuzz with voices.

I took a few steps inside and immediately came back out. As I came out, I noticed that there was a guard at the entrance. I returned to the car and asked Sahadeo to accompany me. It seemed as if he didn't understand me for a moment, but the very next second, he said, 'Oh! Okay.' As he got out of the car, he asked, 'What are you getting me into, mister?'

From what Anasuya had said, I thought there would be more people. But as I walked into the station once more, I saw that there were only four, including her. They stood facing the police station as if it was a temple, with a sense of supplication. Two constables blocked their path at the threshold. One stood with his back against a pillar, head turned up towards the skies and eyes closed. The other sat on the threshold, the folds in his neck shifting as he looked at them in turn. He kept saying he was listening to them, but he was the only one speaking. His legs were spread wide, and he had pressed his lathi – a well-oiled, gleaming bamboo stick, I should add – into the ground between them, as if he wanted to drill to the centre of the earth.

The three men accompanying Anasuya could easily be identified, not just because they were young, but also because they looked agitated. Anasuya had a hand on her hip, as if it was the only way she was able to stand. She wore a faded green salwar-suit with a turquoise dupatta folded twice and meticulously draped around herself.

I was watching this as I came forward. Then something happened that I would never have believed had it not occurred right in front of me.

Let me first address the matter of belief. Why wouldn't I have believed it? Was it because, despite being a writer, I believed in systems and organizations more than in human beings? Or was it because I had so far been spared by this organization known as the police? Why?

That ruffian, sorry, that constable who sat on the threshold, picked up his lathi and poked its lower end, which had some mud stuck to it, against Anasuya's belly. Twisting it hard, he asked menacingly, 'How far along?'

All three young men shouted at once, and the two constables were perhaps just waiting for the chance. The thuds of the lathis began to drown out the cacophony of abuses. But what was truly heart-wrenching were the screams that rang out between the blows. Were there two criminals and three human beings, or two policemen and three criminals? How could I watch this? How was the world watching it?

I ran towards the commotion. Sahadeo raced ahead of me, and some others too. But they stopped at a little distance. If I say that the constables stopped beating them because we ran towards the men, it would not just be a lie but also an act of ingratitude. But they stopped. Sahadeo went over to the students while I went to Anasuya. Several others watched her with such timid helplessness, as if they would have done anything for her, if only they could. When I saw that there were a few women among the crowd who would take care of her, I left her side and walked up to the constables.

I tried to remember where else I had witnessed a scene similar to the one I had just seen – of the constable pushing his lathi into Anasuya's belly. But in that terrifying moment, I couldn't remember where. I did not know how to talk to the police. I did not even know how to address them. The idea of giving them respect and calling them 'sir' was abhorrent. If I said, 'Good morning,' they would know I was an outsider. So, I simply joined my hands and said, 'Namaskar.'

The two sat on the threshold, panting. When they saw me, one of them said, 'Bark.'

'Ji, namaskar. My name is Arjun. I am her husband's friend.'

The act of uttering this sentence alone drenched me in sweat. If there was a mirror in front of me, I would have seen the drops pop out on my forehead. But there was only the grimy wall of the law, and all I could see was fear. In that mirror of fear, all I could see was Anasuya sitting on the ground with her legs splayed out. As for myself, I just felt like I had been shoved into a deep well from the mountain peak that was Delhi.

'Ji, I am her husband's friend. I've come from Delhi.'

Perhaps it would have been better not to mention Delhi, but it would have inevitably come up sooner or later. Nonetheless, they must have felt I was trying to throw my weight around by bringing up my big-city background right at the beginning. If they didn't panic, it was well and good. But if they did, they could have hurt us all. So, I changed the topic and reconciled myself to addressing the two criminals as 'sir'.

'Sir, I am Rafique's friend.'

'Will you say something else?' The two spoke up at once.

'Sir, he hasn't come home for three days.'

'Are you his lawyer?'

'Not at all, sir. I am just a friend. I come from Delhi, where I work for a publishing house.' I tried to keep the mood light, but I didn't know how long I could continue with this.

'Are you a writer?' a third constable who sat a little apart asked, almost shouting out his question. I was so focused on the first two, I wouldn't even have realized he was present had he not interrupted. This would have been extremely difficult to answer, but fortunately one of the policemen at the threshold asked, 'Which newspaper?'

I calmly responded, 'Sir, Niyamgiri is a publishing house. It also has a post called "editor", which is more like that of a clerk and nowhere near as powerful as that of a newspaper editor. I am an editor with Niyamgiri.'

I was astonished. What had happened to my self-confidence? What about me being a writer? Where did my faith in the power of words go? Why was I afraid? And if I was afraid, then why was that fear spreading through my words?

The third constable walked up to us, taking his time to climb down the two steps just so he could smile.

'Daroga Babu will come sometime between 3.30 and 5. A Union minister is visiting in a few days and we have to make preparations. Most of us at the station are busy with that. Come back in the afternoon. The matter can be registered only then. Explain this to your friend's family as well.' He came right up to me as he said this.

His words came as a relief. I was so glad to get over my agony that I told them I would come back in the afternoon and helped the students get up. Those who saw me may have thought I was helping them because the beating had broken them. But the reality was something else. I couldn't understand how I would face Anasuya. We were meeting each other after eleven or twelve years. And I still couldn't make up my mind whether to continue carrying the ghosts of our past, or to start anew, like a friend who had come to provide her succour in her time of trouble. Or should I be like a stranger, trying superficially to soothe her pain? These questions slammed me over and over as if I was stuck inside a broken lift.

I stopped thinking about all this because I still needed to look after Anasuya. I turned around. She sat so still, even a stone could have taken lessons from her. I remembered her eyes, but at this moment they were brimming, like an ocean that one cannot fathom or even gaze into. When she closed her eyes, copious tears streamed out. When she opened them, the teardrops hung from her eyelashes the way raindrops hang from a clothesline. She continued to blink hard, as if she couldn't decide whether to keep her eyes open or closed. There was no third option, after all.

Two women helped her up before I could reach her. They too must have come to the station because of some compulsion. I gestured to one of them to step aside and held Anasuya's arm. That's when Anasuya looked at me, and I looked at her looking at me. It must not have been more than a few moments, and god knows what she saw, but what I saw was a cobweb of bygone memories. Sahadeo rushed to the car. Anasuya gestured as if to tell me she didn't need assistance. I was relieved she didn't push me away. I let go of her arm but motioned to the woman walking by her side to carry on.

I thought I must speak to the constables once more. If they agreed to register an FIR for a bribe, I should pay them. But what if they got riled by my offer? Policemen do not refuse a bribe, I was sure. Why would anyone think otherwise? But if the act of bribing them brought with it the risk of them getting caught, it would aggravate them. When I turned around, I found the third constable standing right in front of me. The two of us were not even a metre apart. If I were a child, I would have wet my pants. He shot off, 'Are you a writer?'

A black badge on the right of his uniform announced his name: 'Brijnandan'.

I replied, 'What are you saying, sir?' What else could I have said?

He asked once more, his voice insistent this time. 'Are you?'

I was aware of the pitfalls of such a situation. If the police sensed they needed to be careful about something, it would hurt the matter of Rafique's investigation one way or another. For this reason, and since I had not written for a while, I simply said: 'No.'

The car was parked right outside the police station's gate. I was about a hundred feet away, but I could see Anasuya sitting in the back seat, spent. Once again, I asked myself whether I had ever seen a policeman pushing a lathi against a woman's stomach before – and if I had, where had I seen it? This was the first time I was engaged with a matter involving the police, so where could I have witnessed such a scene? Was it in a film?

It was clear from the constables' attitude that they had little interest in looking for Rafique. Perhaps none at all. Was this an indication of imminent misery, or a misgiving buried deep in my subconscious? Or perhaps a general carelessness was behind their lack of interest. After all, they were not even filing Rafique's disappearance as a case.

Here I must inform you, dear reader, that I do not know how to respond to situations. I have always been in awe of those who can gather their words and emotions, and respond in an appropriate manner. For example, I cannot go to a grieving person and say, 'I am very sorry for what has happened, but god will help you.' Since most can do this, I wouldn't judge my reaction as right or wrong. But I personally feel that even turning up at an event of joy or sorrow and standing by someone when the situation calls for it is a message in itself. The gesture withers as soon as you try to put it in words. But then, the whole world does it, so who's to say?

The car door opened. Anasuya furrowed her brows at the sound but kept her eyes closed. I asked the three students how they had come. They pointed to their bicycles. Sahadeo motioned for me to take a seat. I sat in the front and cast a glance towards the station. The three constables were staring at us. Sahadeo turned on the engine. I got out of the front seat, walked around the car, opened the back door, and got in. The whole world does it, after all.

WHEN PEOPLE MEET, THEIR COMING together builds on the course of all their previous meetings. But how nice it would be if meetings could be devoid of memories! The degree of familiarity between one human being and another also presents a further complication. If the woman sitting next to me were my wife, sister or mother, would I be so helpless in consoling her? The past should not hurt this bad. Do only human beings have this feeling of unfamiliarity, or do other species feel it too?

I began with a terse question. 'What happened?'

She tossed her head back and didn't respond. I was about to ask another question, when it struck me that, try as we might to suppress our memories of others for many years or presume that we have erased them from our minds, we forget that they're just lurking around the corner, waiting for a signal to reappear. That day, I began to believe that the first human revolutions were built on memories. Because a decades-old phrase, a private code, suddenly came to me and I said, 'Look ahead.'

She looked at me. The past materialized in front of us like an awful carbon copy. Or like a piece of writing on paper whose ink had begun to fade. I remembered that magicians' act, where they write on a blank page but no words appear until they hold it up against a lit matchstick.

She has been waiting at Karnal's Liberty Chowk for a while. She is the daughter of my landlord. Whenever we have to meet outside, she leaves home first, and I leave fifteen or twenty minutes later. She thinks she has had to wait longer. Our plan is to see the entire city of Delhi on my motorcycle. But she is upset, because a girl from our neighbourhood saw me flirting with her and could now play spoilsport by telling on us.

She hops on to the pillion seat. Because she is upset, she doesn't even lean on my shoulder, let alone hold me by my waist. But she sits right behind me. When I want to get down, she says, 'Look ahead.' When I slow down the motorbike and try to tell her something, she says, 'Look ahead.' We don't speak until we reach Sukhdeo's dhaba. My misery is mounting. We stop for tea. I know she likes hers with milk, but I want to gauge her mood, so I ask, 'Milk tea?'

Once again, she says, 'Look ahead.' But this time, she is laughing.

The phrase comes to be used by both of us on various occasions, often when we do not have any other way out. When I accept my job transfer against her wishes, 'look ahead' comes to the rescue that day too.

I sit in her room. Her parents are not home, nor are her two brothers who bay for my blood. She sits down slowly. We don't know yet how the transfer will affect us. For now, we are arguing about whether I should accept the transfer or quit my job and look for another. She holds my face in her hands, turns it towards her, and says, 'Look ahead.' I look at her. The memory of that moment will continue to haunt me through the rest of my life. But I do not know that yet.

The town was less than a kilometre away from the police station. It seemed to be lost in itself. Everyone looked as if they were occupied with something. Besides the many makeshift kiosks on the streets, the first store in the town was an electric sawmill, the noise from which could be heard from far away. The town grew crowded immediately after the mill. Sahadeo must have been feeling uneasy at the growing silence inside the car, so he said, 'Sir, Bihar starts right after this settlement.'

He must have been familiar with this place and that is why he called it a 'settlement'. I had been calling it a 'town'.

'What do you mean "Bihar starts from here"?'

'It's a paradise for smugglers and criminals, from that side and from this side too. If a new police chief comes on either side of the border, the miscreants cross over.'

I didn't say anything but let out a laugh at this creative use of borders. Had Anjan Agarwal used the same technique to his benefit? The thought was a distraction and it got me to look outside the car. There were lots of hoardings and jostling banners on both sides of the street. Every hoarding was perhaps twenty-five to fifty metres apart. One advertised various discounts at Big Bazaar, but in blue and not the sparkling red that had become associated with the outlet. Only when we drove past it did I notice that the advert was for *Bigger* Bazaar and not Big Bazaar. It was a great imitation. Right behind it was a hoarding for a computer repair store that said in big letters: 'A computer doctor, now in your town'. The text for the advertisement was replete with medical jargon. In fact, on the top-left corner of the hoarding, there was even a photograph of a man wearing a doctor's white coat standing next to a computer screen.

The next hoarding had a random assortment of bright colours, and I couldn't discern it very well. But after two or three more of these, it became clear that the people whose photos were featured on these hoardings were all the same. On the top were ten or twelve photos without any names. I could only recognize Swami Vivekananda. On his right were pictures of the Prime Minister and other Union ministers. Text had been stacked to the left and in the centre. One hoarding announced a pilgrimage to Kailash–Mansarovar. 'Chalo Kailash!' – Let's go to Kailash! – the large type called out. A huge image of Lord Shiva was printed alongside, with the Ganga flowing out from his locks. To the right of the god, almost as big or perhaps bigger, was a photograph of a young man whose entire manner seemed calculated to convey humility and sincerity. Below his picture, typed in yellow letters, was his name and official position: 'Amit Malviya – President, Mangal Morcha'.

The choice of colours could make one wonder if the banners had been put up in a great hurry. But the order in which they had been placed revealed that this was not the case. If the call for the pilgrimage was on the right side of the street, the same hoarding was on the left too – in the same size, with the same colour, people and text. The coordination was perfect. Even the hoardings that were put up right after repeated the message. Whoever had done this clearly did not want a single person passing by on the street to miss it.

A bhandara – a religious feast – was advertised on the next hoarding. It was similar in type and colour to the Kailash one, so it was not difficult to guess what it said. As the car came near it, I saw that the feast would go on for a week. The same photos were printed on the top, starting from Swami Vivekananda and ending with the Prime Minister. But while Lord Shiva had towered over the previous one, here it was the goddess Annapurna. The designer had been astute enough to add the deity's name, given that she was not as popular as Shiva. Two photographs were printed to its right: one of Amit Jain – Treasurer, Mangal Morcha, and the other of Amit Malviya. These hoardings had been arranged in the same way too: front-back-right-left, four in all.

The next hoarding advertised a pilgrimage to Vaishno Devi and Amarnath. If you ignored the many photos, it looked like the cover of an old T-Series album.

The one after that advertised a private university. The letters 'BL(D)U' were printed in large type, and the name followed in parentheses, 'Baba Lakarnath (Deemed) University'. The photographs of two boys and a girl, all three wearing formal suits, were placed next to it. I couldn't tell whether they were students at the college or professional models. The girl wore a collarless shirt, while the boys wore ties. The advertisement said admissions into courses like Management, Hotel Management, BEd, BSc, MSc, BCom, MCom, BA, MA, etc. were about to close soon, and to reserve a seat as early as possible. A phone number had been listed for enquiries, and on the corner to its right were small photographs of two men. The word 'Principal' was typed below one, with the name following in a very small font. Or perhaps I couldn't read it because there was already so much text on the advert. The other photo was that of an older man with a glowing face, and below it were listed several academic degrees and awards. The awards looked to be of the literary kind, but our car had already zipped past the hoarding before I could read his name.

There was a traffic jam up ahead. Everybody had squeezed their vehicles in wherever they found some space, and now several cars were stuck on both sides. An Indica stood sideways. An autorickshaw's front wheel popped out towards the right. Everybody honked relentlessly. Anasuya watched the mayhem. Thinking this could be a chance to start a conversation, I asked, 'What sort of traffic jam is this?' Then, 'Does this happen every day?'

She responded to both my questions with a terse, 'I never come this way.'

As I wondered whether to keep the conversation going, Sahadeo changed the topic and said this was where smugglers paid toll tax. 'A government checkpoint comes after crossing the river Gandak in Mehrauna,' he said, 'where vehicles carrying legal goods are checked. But in Noma, the tax is paid by smugglers. Oil, cattle and sugar are all trafficked via this route, and one has to pay to smuggle out or bring in every sack of sugar or head of cattle. The rates are quite high these days. This is the gateway to our state.'

He had begun to irritate me with his stories, so I asked him to keep quiet. There was no point in believing what he said.

'Take the right from Durga Mandir Chowk please,' Anasuya said in a calm voice. I had been waiting for this moment. At some point, the tears dry up, despair leaves your side, and anger fades away. This relief doesn't last for very long – anger often returns with renewed vigour, and the tears return too. But I had been waiting for this interval of respite, even if it was just for a moment or two.

After giving directions to Sahadeo, Anasuya rummaged inside a yellow plastic bag that had 'Furkan Vastralaya' printed on it and brought out another plastic bag that had been folded several times. Water dripped from it. As she unfolded the bag, it continued to drip. Sahadeo watched the scene unfold in his rear-view mirror. He would have minded if the seat got wet, and I didn't want that to happen. The deeper we went into town, the more I felt like going back home. But I wouldn't have found another taxi in this town-like settlement – or settlement-like town.

Anasuya brought out four objects from the bag that, had they not been drenched, could have been called diaries or notebooks. The paper had swollen. She handed them to me and said, 'When the police raided our home, I rolled up Rafique's diary, his notebook and two photocopies of his new play in this bag and hid them in the flush tank. This is the best I could do. I folded the plastic bag several times, but water still got in.'

I took the papers as a courtesy, also thinking that this might somehow start a conversation. A few pages became casualties in this exchange. As I put them back inside the yellow plastic bag, I said something I wished I hadn't: 'Was Rafique involved in politics?'

Who would have answered such a ridiculous question? She certainly didn't.

We had arrived at her home.

Her house looked more like a cage. It was no wider than twelve to fifteen feet, however long it may have been from the inside. The other houses in this neighbourhood, which was close to the centre of Noma, all looked the same.

Sahadeo hurried ahead of me to open the door for Anasuya so that she had no trouble getting down. Noticing the taxi, Anasuya's landlord came out. He took one look at our gloomy faces and didn't bother asking what had happened. Nonetheless, Anasuya told him at once, 'We've been asked to come back once the daroga returns in the afternoon.' The landlord's wife helped her climb upstairs. Every step seemed to be as hard as climbing a mountain for Anasuya. She would take one step, then bring up the other foot. She would then take a deep breath and repeat the exercise.

After climbing more than half the stairs, she seemed to remember that I had been left behind. 'Come up,' she invited me in.

It was a one-room apartment. The hundred-watt bulb's luminescence couldn't overpower the enormous darkness inside. If the bulb wasn't lit, I wouldn't be able to see my hands. There was a kitchen in one corner of the room, and you could see the bathroom through an open door on the far end. The bed was simply a mattress on the floor, facing west. There was only one chair and she asked me to sit on it, but I offered it to the landlord instead. Anasuya slowly lowered herself on to the bed. The landlord's wife sat with her, put Anasuya's feet in her lap and massaged them slowly. I stood with the three students – Jagdish, Kushalpal and Mukesh.

I looked at the three youngsters. How, instead of looking to the future, they were stuck watching the handiwork of previous generations. The room was not big enough to accommodate so many people. It was also difficult to understand why a teacher from a degree college was living in such conditions.

The walls were empty – not even a single picture hung from them – and made me yearn for a glimpse of Rafique.

'Do you have any photos of Rafique?'

Anasuya looked towards her purse lying a little further away. All of us followed her gaze, and Jagdish picked up the purse and handed it to her. The purse was the colour of a banyan tree's bark. Old and battered, only its purse-like shape gave any indication of its function. Anasuya took out four pictures from it.

The first picture looked like it had been clicked at some ceremony. The photo had lost its lustre over time. A young woman had put a garland around a man's neck and now waited for the man to put one around hers. Both of them looked into the camera as if someone had asked to click a picture at that very moment. Two young women and a man laughed behind them.

The second picture had the shine of a new photo and seemed to have been clicked at dusk. A scene from a street play that had been shot at a wide angle. The young man who had looked eager to place the garland in the previous picture was now being held by a policeman. Kushal, one of the three students who stood with me, played the policeman. A young woman looked on, afraid at what was going on around her.

The third student, Mukesh, came closer. Putting his finger on the young woman's face, he said, 'Her name is Janaki. She too has been missing since yesterday.' He stumbled through the sentence, which may have been because of his choice of words. 'I mean, she has not returned home since yesterday,' he clarified.

I told them I had read about her in *Dainik Jagriti*. Everybody turned to look at me.

Janaki–Rafique, Rafique–Janaki. My mind raced around the two names. I almost asked how long the two had known each other – and how well. The query settled itself in a narrow corner of my mind, or rather, in a corner of my narrow mind. But I could not resist asking, 'Is Janaki one of Rafique's students?'

A wave of silence enveloped the room and would have overpowered us all had Anasuya not answered – plainly and simply, but her expression was remarkable. The sternness with which she said 'yes' could have set to rest any future questions too. 'She even comes home every now and then.

She is part of their theatre group, and these three were also part of the same street play in the photograph.' The three nodded. Mukesh began to tell me about the play. They had decided to start performing it from the end of May, but their scheduled performances had been blocked because of some civic issues. Jagdish corrected some details. But I kept returning to the question of the two going missing at the same time.

The third photo was a passport-sized one and, from a distance, looked like it had been taken from the admit card of an exam, for the marks of a stamp and a faded signature were visible too. But the picture had been cut out from a larger photograph. On a closer look, it seemed as if it had been subjected to inks of various colours.

I could not figure out whether the fourth and last picture depicted a play or reality. The same young man, this time in a gown worn at convocations, was receiving a degree from an elderly man. The picture could very well have been real, except there was no one else in the photograph. Which was possible only if it had been clicked up-close, or if it were a scene from a play.

Jagdish asked for my WhatsApp number. It was clear that he wanted to send me Rafique's pictures. I handed all four to him.

Then, I finally uttered the sentence I had been preparing to say for a long time. 'I want to know a few more things from you.' Anasuya gestured at me to stop. She closed her eyes. After a short pause, she said, 'We will talk.' I was walking out without having heard what she'd said, when she mumbled, 'Wait.'

❖

'Tea?'

'No.'

I, however, liked the idea. The whoosh of the gas burner and the simmering of the tea leaves would allow us a chance to recoup. Otherwise, was this really any way to meet?

She pointed towards the kitchen. The stove was on the floor. I lit it with a matchstick and started boiling the water. 'Tell me what happened?'

She took her own time before she started to speak. 'I might be able to say something if I could figure things out myself. Everything was fine at college. Rafique has been teaching at Swami Devanand Degree College for the last five years, and sometimes he talks about his ad-hoc job. Some people in the college feel that he is doing well despite being an ad-hoc teacher, so he would have a reasonable chance of getting a permanent position when it opens up. That's why they want him to quit. They create problems every year during the new appointments. Rafique has mentioned a few confrontations. But I can't believe they would go to such an extent.'

I could believe it, however. Jobs were more precious than lives nowadays. If it was me, I would not have dismissed their possible involvement in Rafique's disappearance.

If it was me? What did I mean by that? What did it require for me to say, 'It *is* me'? I could beat myself up for my habit of running away from the present. But I was here now. Very much here, and no one would be excluded from my list of suspects until Rafique was found. This town, its people, nobody would get any leeway.

'Did Rafique ever tell you the names of those with whom he had a confrontation?'

'Jagdish and Kushal would know more about this, but there is someone called Guru-ji – a man named Ratnashankar Mishra. He used to come home earlier.'

I didn't insist on that point. There was so much else that I wanted to know. Most of all, I wanted to know who had suffered more after I had left her stranded. It was an unreasonable question, and I chided myself for thinking about the past when there were lives at stake here.

'How did you end up in Noma? This town is the complete opposite of Karnal's glitter.'

She started to laugh, but her weariness did not allow her to do so properly. She tried to say something but kept laughing over and over. I realized I should have framed the question differently. 'You had two brothers, didn't you?'

She patiently began to reply. And she said the same things I had been thinking about since the previous night. But to be honest, it didn't feel good to hear her say them.

'My brothers didn't like our relationship.' It would have been enough, had she stopped at this point. But she thought it necessary to continue speaking – as if her monologue would help solve the mess she was in and help find Rafique. A constant undertone of bitterness was now discernible in her words. Her face turned red. Her anger was justified.

Someone whose husband has gone missing has every right to see the world as a bad place. The only problem was that I was also a character in her tale. I listened to her. Finding Rafique now became all the more necessary because I had started fearing guilt as much as I feared committing a crime.

'It took you seven or eight years to understand that you wanted a girl from your own caste, but I had figured it out fairly early. Your actions told me everything. You did not have the courage to say no, and that is why you dragged the relationship on, and demoralized me for one reason or another. You know, after breaking up with you, I swear on my mother, I didn't feel any further grief. I met Rafique around the same time. He had been appointed, albeit temporarily, to Kurukshetra University. You may be surprised to learn we decided to get married after just two or three meetings. But my brothers didn't like him either. They wanted to kill him and nearly beat me to death.' She started to cry. 'Rafique left Haryana. Some friends helped us find this town and this place. And a job. Which was supposed to be permanent from day one but has remained temporary for the last five years.'

I kept quiet.

'Got it? And yes, if the police register an FIR, I will certainly add my brothers' names. Understand?'

Her exhaustion caused her words to dry up. Her tongue and lips were not working in tandem. Saliva dripped out of her mouth, but she continued to talk. Her last statement did not carry the baggage of her previous outburst, nor was she trying to appease me. There was only a desolate, broken bridge that could have joined the two of us, if at all. There was nothing to do but to look ahead.

'If your brothers wanted to do something, why would they wait for five or six years?'

'You waited for seven or eight years too, didn't you? What harm had I done to you?'

She began to cry inconsolably. She was crying for Rafique. There was no question of crying for me, or over her past. As her sobs overpowered her, she started calling out Rafique's name. Her mourning was also for the loneliness society had gifted her on her marriage. I remembered an experience of being boycotted by society, though only for a brief period, in my childhood. I could understand that Anasuya had been rendered so alone that she had lost herself as well. She wept so much that the three students came in. I stood, walked up to her and rubbed her forehead. I rubbed her forehead and helped her lie down. Even as she lay down hiccupping, she kept calling out Rafique's name.

If I had to grab hold of a thread to make sense of the tale I found myself in, I knew it would have to start from her home. I also knew I was out of my depth. My complacence advised me over and over to run away from this conundrum. But the same complacence also dictated that I stay around Anasuya at that moment. It told me that whoever I was within my own shell, that person was different from the self-absorbed man who sat next to the pregnant woman whose Rafique had gone missing. Or rather, had been made to go missing.

Who was this Rafique?

Oh, sorry, who *is* this Rafique?
Who?

I sent a message to Archana telling her I may have to stay in Noma for a few more days, then kept staring at the screen.

A look outside was enough to tell me the time. The sun blazed. It was very hot, and terribly humid too. Everyone was quiet. I had the landlord, Jagdish, Kushalpal and Mukesh for company. Sahadeo was dozing in his taxi downstairs. When the landlord asked about lunch, I was reminded of another important question. 'Is there a hotel or lodge here to stay?'

The landlord mentioned Adarsh Hotel.

Radha Chitra Mandir was the only cinema hall in town. On its right was a narrow alley, and the third building in this alley was Adarsh Hotel. We had to go to the police station at 3.30 p.m., and because they were hungry, I had asked the three students to come along with me. If you keep walking down this alley, you will reach the western gate of Swami Devanand Degree College, they told me. I thought about going to the college and talking to Rafique's colleagues and other students to understand him. But my face-off with the system that day had already exhausted me, and I thought it better to go to the hotel.

The reception was underneath the staircase. There were two big registers on that long table. There wasn't enough light here either. The boy behind the desk had been sitting so low that when I knocked on the desk, he emerged as if out of the earth's womb. He held a book, which comforted and confused me. I couldn't understand this town. Jagdish asked him, 'When did you start reading, bhai?' The question boomeranged on him, for Mukesh and Kushalpal countered, 'How do you know him? Do you come here lots?' Jagdish did not reply.

The boy at the reception announced that both electricity and the police could arrive here at any time, without warning. I would have to show my identity card. When I said I'd put down my name and address in the register, he grew upset and said doing so would cost me 800 rupees for a room. If I stayed without registering, it would cost me 500 rupees.

The boy came along to show me the room. There was no place for drivers to sleep, but he said several rooms were unoccupied and he could make arrangements for Sahadeo in one of them. Even better – I understood that tea and food would have to be ordered from outside. But what took the cake was when the boy told me I was the first guest at the hotel to come from out of town in the last two years.

At least he gave me a clean bed.

'What does Rafique teach you?'

'He mostly takes undergraduate classes. He has taught us Surdas's devotional poems and Premchand's stories. He hadn't been given any postgraduate classes, but ever since Radheshyam Shukla took ill, he was assigned to teach Tulsidas too.'

'Not *was* assigned, *has been* assigned.'

'I'm sorry, has been assigned.'

I was annoyed with myself – at my ridiculous questions and the equally ridiculous answers. What did I want to know? Where is Rafique? Then why wasn't I asking directly? But who could I ask?

I spoke to the three of them again: 'What do you guys think? Did Rafique go somewhere on his own? Or has he met with a mishap? Did he have any enemies?'

All three started to reply at the same time, but Kushalpal's voice was louder so the others stopped. 'He can't possibly have any enemies. Our Rafique Sir is an artist. He wasn't planning to go anywhere. We have a performance in four days, he is the director...'

He hadn't even finished when a ruckus from the road outside the hotel sucked out every sound from the room. All of us rushed down and saw an elderly man yelling at Sahadeo. The parked taxi had virtually blocked the alley. I did not wish for any more trouble, so I apologized to the man and requested Sahadeo to park the taxi along the main road. I would call him when we had to go somewhere.

I had been surrounded by people since morning, and now I yearned for solitude. Solitude to let me think about what to do next. Solitude so that I could look at myself in a mirror and ask whether my spineless act of bending over for the policemen could be considered human. I did not know I was such a coward. As a matter of fact, I was certainly not as cowardly when it came to my own safety. But in the world of my beliefs, there was no place to scare or be scared.

I looked into the mirror.

It was quite clear that the habit of taking shortcuts and cutting corners to get the job done had eroded my personality. And I had been encouraging this erosion by calling it politeness. The result was that I ended up grovelling in places where I needed to be an equal.

This thought also troubled me because my unholy submission in front of the constables would affect Anasuya's morale, and the morale of those three students who were supposed to be warriors of the future.

Water dripped on to the bed as soon as I opened the yellow plastic bag that had Rafique's diary, his notebook and other papers. The diary's cover had also swelled up. It was from the year 2013. It was brown and carried an image of two hands joined together. When I tried to pry it open, two wet pages fell out. The ink had run all over the pages, but it was possible to read the writing towards the top. The page was dated 17 April 2015. I realized Rafique had used an old diary by writing a new date on it. I had done this too, but only when there were too many diaries and if one had been used sparingly in the year it was meant for. I used them to make notes.

Two sentences were missing from Rafique's writing where the ink had been washed out. It was difficult to infer whether they had gone for a test from the hospital. The words and letters that I could understand were:

> *17/4/15*
> *The doctor has said no more rickshaws. I have also said no to that. I don't want her to ride even an*

autorickshaw. The doctor says that, for the next two months, Anasuya should not ride any vehicle that does not have shock absorbers. The next test recommended by Doctor Madam can only be done in Deoria or Gorakhpur. She has a misgiving that the foetus – Why should I call it a foetus? It may be a foetus for the doctor, but for me it is my child – is not showing enough activity ********* Before Anasuya assumes surveillance mode, on my way to college tomorrow I will have to remind Madhusudan from R.K. Agency about the money they owe me.

I put aside the soaked and tattered diary and saw that it was already 2 p.m. I waded through my entire phonebook. Looking for some relief, I dug out the names of a few people I could talk to about the problems here and ask for help. But before I could call anyone, the owner of the publishing house where I worked called me. I told him everything without hesitation. There was no need to conceal the fact that I had been Anasuya's friend, and that I had to submit myself in front of the policemen this morning. In fact, I emphasized this. I repeated it twice. The third time, I told him the act was utterly unacceptable to me, no matter what anyone else thought.

He heard me out, then asked for Rafique's name, the name of his college, Noma's name, Deoria's name, and Gorakhpur's name – twice. After listening to everything, he assured me, 'Someone will call you.' Then he said, 'If there is any problem, Arjun, inform me right away.'

I had criticized him in the past for using his political connections, but perhaps they would prove useful for me today.

We could call him 'daroga' for our own convenience, but what he had been appointed to was the magical post of 'circle officer'. One could get a sense of his imposing height even as he sat on his chair. And when he got up in an attempt to welcome us, it became clear that he was at least six and a half feet tall. He wore a half-sleeved shirt that fit him snugly. He had a polite way of speaking, and one could say that he was good looks personified. His name was Shalabh Shrinet.

The sun continued to beat down relentlessly.

When I entered the front yard of the station, my cowardly behaviour from the morning began to play before my eyes, scene by scene, as if I was watching a rerun. Everything unfolded once more – the people, the conversations, even the breeze in the air and the proportion of light and shade. I did not wish to see those three constables again when I entered the station. Just my luck, though – all three of them sat right there. We exchanged looks, but even they pretended as if the morning's events had never happened, as if we had never met, as if they had never shoved the lathi against Anasuya's stomach, as if I had never grovelled in front of them, as if such things were not even possible.

But the last link in this series of as-ifs – *as if Rafique had never gone missing* – was absent.

There was a platform under a peepul tree, on which was written: 'Wednesday, weekly issue-settlement day.' Four policemen sat there with a young Sikh man. They seemed to be having a laugh about something. It didn't look like the Sikh man was an outsider. Rafique's students smiled when they saw him. He raised a hand in return. Kushalpal went up to greet him and returned after a momentary exchange of pleasantries.

We were around ten or eleven people, including Anasuya. She was asked to sit on the chair across from the daroga, but she sat on a bench to the side. Five students had come along this time. There were three of Rafique's colleagues, the landlord, and me. Rafique's colleagues introduced themselves. They had come upon the insistence of the students. Two of them, Arvind Srivastava and Rohitashva, taught Hindi, while the third gentleman, Sadanand Mishra, was from the mathematics department. There wasn't enough space for all of us to sit. The daroga insisted several times that I sit, but I respectfully declined.

The conversation had to start from somewhere, so he began, 'Can you believe it? Such a big author is in our city and nobody knows about it?' Not getting the enthusiastic reaction he had perhaps expected, he rallied again, 'We must get you felicitated,' in a manner indicating that the teachers should join him.

This was preposterous. In the literary world, the act of felicitation was always spoken of in the third person.

'So-and-so has been felicitated by so-and-so.' Today, however, the condescending statement had been thrown at me. I knew he was a daroga. He knew he was one too. But just so that he didn't doubt I was aware of whether he was a daroga or not, I thought it was the perfect time to respond to his niceties and his attempts at breaking the ice. 'Sir, please find Rafique. That by itself would be felicitation enough for all of us. Look at this woman. She is seven months along and is running from pillar to post just to get an FIR registered.'

He seemed to have heard just one word from my monologue: 'sir'.

'Please don't call me "sir",' he said.

I didn't let him finish, and raising my tone by a little so that everybody could hear me, albeit remaining respectful and polite, I said, 'Sir, you deserve to be called "sir", that's why I am calling you "sir". The police are society's armour. You work for the nation as much as the army does on our borders. The tales of your bravery and struggles can be found in folklore and books.' I had no idea what I was saying.

He interrupted me. 'Don't call our struggles "tales", mister. They're the truth. Writing tales is what *you* people do.' I thought my monologue had backfired, but he laughed it away. I could have gone on and on, but between glances at a file, he asked Anasuya, 'Do you also know Janaki?'

Anasuya looked at everyone one by one, as if to ascertain whether what just happened had really happened or not. Then she said, 'Yes.'

'That girl's father had also filed a missing-person report yesterday. Your husband – what do you people call a husband, "shauhar", right? – since when has he not come home?'

'I came to the police station thrice yesterday. I spent almost the whole day here.'

'Since when has he not come home?'

'Saturday.'

The daroga looked at the third constable and said, 'And today is Monday.' He then addressed me, 'Sir, the police have been doing their work.' Then he addressed us all, 'Kindly write an application.' He then turned back to the third constable. 'Brijnandan-ji, kindly do the "receiving".' Turning towards Anasuya, he said, 'The police will do its job, but do you suspect anyone?' Then he asked me, 'How do you know her?'

Without waiting for anyone's reply, he then told Anasuya, 'Our initial investigations have found that your family, especially your two brothers, were opposed to your marriage and you came here to escape their ire.' He walked up to me and motioned to join him outside as he went out into the garden.

Three chairs had been placed outside. The daroga – Shalabh – faced the garden. As he was talking to me, he smiled back at every passer-by's greetings. I could see inside the station from where I sat. The people who had accompanied us were slowly starting to come out. I could see them getting busy with their phones or talking to each other. I could also see that Anasuya was still sitting on the same bench but trying to lean as far as possible in order to be able to look outside. Her eyes were just like I remembered them.

'What do you think? Where could this man have disappeared?' the daroga asked me.

'Sir, this is exactly what I want to know from you. What can remain hidden from the police...'

'You writers are always displeased with the police.'

'I don't believe in such generalizations.'

'You may have spoken to Rafique's neighbours, his wife?' He didn't pause for my reply and continued, 'Both of them are brave. Otherwise, who marries outside of their religion?'

To respond to this would have forced the conversation to take an absurd turn, so I didn't.

He returned to his earlier question: 'How do you know them?'

'Anasuya is my friend.'

'But hadn't you said this morning that you were friends with her – what do these people call it – shauhar?'

I heard someone greeting him with a salute and a 'Jai Hind, sir' from behind us. Must be a policeman, I thought, and turned around to see that it was the second constable from the morning. The same one I had grovelled before. 'Tea and snacks are ready to be served whenever you say, sir,' he said. Hearing the daroga say 'quickly', he turned right back.

The daroga continued, 'If a thread connects the disappearances of both Rafique and Janaki, your presence here could be misconstrued.'

I caught his drift. I smiled and asked him patiently, 'Were you only told what I had said this morning?'

'Did something else happen as well?'

'Will an FIR be registered or not?' I asked again.

He didn't wish to appear weak. 'We will find him before any kind of paperwork, mister!' he said and stood up. 'Join us for dinner tonight.'

I didn't know what else to do but agree. On the other hand, I wondered what the point of having FIRs was if the police refused to register one. The intervention from my boss seemed to be working and not working at the same time. Or perhaps there was no reason for inviting me to dinner besides the fact that I was in a new and unknown place.

As we were about to leave, a constable handed a copy of our application to Anasuya. It was stamped and had two signatures scribbled on it.

THE SILENCE IN THE HOTEL made me realize I was the only guest. The same boy sat at the reception, busy on his cell phone. I felt like asking for his name but let it be. The stairs were just the right amount of dark for being alone. It was difficult to unlock the door. I kept trying the key, which turned ineffectually, as if its teeth could not grip the ridges inside the lock. Once the door opened, it was equally difficult to lock it.

Among the intertwined pages of Rafique's diary, with the dates all mixed up, were what seemed to be parts of a script or a play. One page had an artistic sentence on it. I call it 'artistic' because a note below the sentence said that the play must have a line of dialogue in this form. The sentence was: 'Jagdish said that Prem said that Kushalpal said that Govind didn't really want to but was saying that the Malviya family perhaps wouldn't want to, so Rajshekhar was saying that we would have to meet Surendra Pratap Malviya-ji to seek permission to perform this play at the Dol Mela, and this meeting would be on the instructions of Chairman Shriramraghav Singh.' The page was dated 7 July 2015.

The second page read:

29/6/15

*It was difficult to find Niyaz's address, and even more
difficult to convince him to see us. We met Amandeep
Singh, who has been fired from his job. In just one
meeting, he seemed to be emerging as the hero. He has
no objections to the fact that we are using his name and
the acts he was involved in for our play.*

*Anuradha's family refused to see us. Kushalpal
talked to them. They have said they will speak over the
phone, whatever the case.*

*May god save Anuradha from this limbo between
life and death!*

*This play will have a dedication at the beginning.
All characters will stand together and commemorate
Anuradha as one.*

What should the title be?

The soggy pages were virtually unreadable. Water had
seeped in so deep that one could not pick out a single
dry page amid all the wet pages whose letters had run
off. Finally, I found three pages that were relatively drier,
although the moisture had left them fragile. They began to
tear at my touch:

15/4/15

*Ratnashankar Guru-ji has become an expert in the art
of insulting. The entire city now knows that he doesn't*

like me. What is perhaps not known is that I don't respect him either. If I did respect him, it would have been impossible to endure this humiliation. It must have been a light moment when I asked him why he needed to use his tongue so much if an armed guard walked with him? Today too he acted in a regrettable manner. Shiksha Sadan is a fair distance away from the cycle stand. The ground is bigger than a stadium, and crossing it has its own charm. When a hot wind blows, for instance, just before noon, I'm always reminded of a scene from a film. Antonio Banderas is crossing a big town square. He is soaked, and naked from above the waist, with a chest as broad as a desert, and drops trickling down his pants in time with his steps. A truck halts as if to salute Banderas's beauty, as if the driver wants to learn something from his gait. I don't remember anything else after this scene, not even the name of the movie, whether it was Desperado *or* Once Upon a Time in Mexico. *But this scene comes to mind whenever I see somebody crossing this ground by themselves. I hope, one day, to make Kushalpal walk across the ground in exactly the same manner while I shoot a video. But today, as I was about to get to my bicycle, I heard someone call out to me with their mouth full of paan. I turned around and saw Ratnashankar Guru-ji standing in his veranda, along with his guard and a few students. His students don't even greet me in his presence, but at least they treat me with a modicum of respect when he is not around. He gestured at me to come to the veranda. I crossed the ground again. But by the time I reached him, he got busy on a call and strolled away. I waited for him along with his students. He returned after forty minutes. The first thing he asked me was, 'Why are you here?' I was not surprised. His students laughed over his behaviour, or perhaps they were just pretending to be amused, it wasn't clear. I said, 'Guru-ji, you called me yourself.' With both disgust and pity in his voice, he responded, 'Why would I call you? You must have misunderstood. Okay, go on now.' Then he joined his students in their banter. I could have responded to him. But what was more important, more than whether or not to respond, was how sensible it would be for me to engage with this pig. I stood there thinking about this when he turned again and asked me, 'Do you have something to say?' I shook my head. 'What could I have to say to you, Guru-ji?' I said and walked away. These frequent insults are becoming unbearable, but who can I talk to about this? It's good that with time, I have lost all respect for most senior teachers, otherwise they would have turned my life into hell.*

We often err in understanding whether it is some divine power that begets violence, or if it's something only us humans do.

17/5/15
The R.K. Agency folks got us to perform a play for the seed company, but when will they pay us? It was

the same old story about a rich farmer versus a poor farmer. Those who used the seeds of that company prospered. I tried to change the characters' names, but the agency was stuck on 'Sukhi Ram' and 'Dukhi Ram'. They have blocked the payment for several months now. I have to see them tomorrow on my way to the college. The company is owned by people related to an influential man like Dadda, but they behave like petty thieves. They have even stopped paying for minor jobs.

All of Anasuya's reports are positive. She is three months along. She thinks it's a boy. I think it's our love.

13/4/15

Have to prepare two of Jon Fosse's plays during the upcoming summer vacation. Kushal, Mukesh and Janaki like Fosse's Girl on the Sofa. *It has plenty of scope for direction. I have to refrain from exercising my veto this time. The play will be selected by the students, but Jagdish and I want to perform* Melancholia. *Let's see what drama takes place over these two dramas in tomorrow evening's meeting.*

My mood turned sour after reading the first few pages. Have those who invented ad-hocism ever paid attention to the appalling conditions of contractual teachers? I was also surprised to learn that despite being on a contract, Rafique had dedicated himself to theatre. This was quite an achievement. It must have taken a lot out of him, to stand tall amid all the hassles, with the desire to do something worthwhile, to cherish the beautiful aspects of life.

But the last entry amazed me. Despite living in a mofussil town like Noma and working as a contractual teacher, Rafique had not only been reading Jon Fosse's works, but also performing them with his students without any fuss.

I wanted to meet Rafique even more now, so that I could see what a genuinely focussed and dedicated individual looked like. Rafique seemed to have appeared as if by magic, at this specific moment when he needed me, as an answer to the unresolved questions of my own life. Or at least that was what it felt like to me.

When I found it impossible to turn to any other page without tearing it, I decided to spread them out and dry every single page from his diary.

I started from the wooden cupboard. Its bottom shelf was the biggest among its three shelves, but it could only accommodate six pages at a time. I managed to dry around twenty pages there. A letter or two, or a few words flashed before my eyes in this process, but I needed to read them in their entirety. I grew restless. I needed more surfaces to spread the pages on.

There were four hangers on the uppermost shelf of the cupboard; my clothes hung from two. I put my clothes on the bed and hung three pages each, one beside the other, on the four hangers. The fan caused some of the pages to flutter – not like feathers, but in their own way, just the way sheets of paper flutter in the wind. This meant that some of the pages had begun drying or had dried already.

Repeating the pattern, I spread the pages of the diary and the notebook on the floor, up to the basin in the washroom. A lot of pages were still left, so I spread them over the bed, leaving me just enough space to sleep. I put pages in sets of two, that is, one over the other on the bed. But there were far too many of them. So, I tied one end of a shirt and a pair of trousers to the window and the other end to the bedpost, turning them into a rope to hang the remaining pages to dry.

The entire room was now filled with letters, words, sentences, their meanings, and above all, with the possibility of Rafique being alive. Or not. This tiring exercise had taken me almost three-quarters of an hour, so I too lay down on the bed as soon as I had finished.

Lying down among these words, I began to feel as if I was a word myself. The thought that I myself could be one among the many words in which I had been trying to find the possibilities that led to Rafique's disappearance terrified me. Missing, lost, disappeared – it could be any one of these, but it wasn't. My mind was not ready to assign these adjectives to Rafique either. There are so many lookout notices one sees about missing people, but before this day, I had never ever realized how inhuman it was to ascribe these adjectives to human beings. These cold words used to describe objects sound grotesque when used for human beings. I could understand this, but at the same time, I could not. To keep human dignity intact, it would be best to say

'Rafique has not come back home yet'. A star of hope resides in this line, one that has not yet risen but we know it's there. People should have the freedom to return home whenever they want. There also needs to be a home to return to – even if it is only in the eyes of a wife or in a couple's desires. With the comforting thought that Rafique at least had people and a home to come back to, sleep encircled me from all sides.

WHEN THE BOY FROM THE reception pressed the doorbell, I feared someone would barge in and see the pages scattered across the room. I got ready and came downstairs, not paying attention to who had come to pick me up. It was Shalabh Shrinet himself. To be honest, my disdain for the police diminished a little because of his act. The jeep had a driver, but Shalabh gestured to him to come using some other means of transport. He made me sit in the front and began to drive himself. By now I was drenched in his largesse, so I could only ask, 'Hope I didn't keep you waiting long?'

I was mostly quiet from then onwards, as Shalabh took over the conversation. Many notable people of the town would be attending the function that evening, he said. 'The preparations for the Dol Mela are ongoing. You may want to meet a few people from the organizing committee.' He probably thought I didn't know about the festival, so he explained in detail. 'The Dol Mela takes place here on the day of Janmashtami. The tradition started in 1918 and has been going on uninterrupted since then. Thousands of people attend the fair. A music festival also takes place. The great flautist Hariprasad Chaurasia has been invited this time.' He continued with a chuckle, 'There will be wrestling as well – both physical and political. I would say, stay on for three more days. See this amazing spectacle of folk culture before you leave. This will be my first time too.'

Then suddenly, he changed the topic and said, 'Had I acted in the movies, things would have been very different today.'

I listened to him, and said 'hmm' or laughed at the right times. It began to dawn on me that I had heard of the Dol Mela earlier too.

He had a palatial house. My first reaction was, 'This is yours!' Perhaps he wanted to hear more compliments, so he said with a hint of embarrassment, 'All because of the blessings of people like you.' The lawn seemed like it could be a golf course. The grass was so soft and flat, as if a film heroine had laid down on it and just gotten up. The languid lamps created an atmosphere of twilight and solitude.

Shalabh asked me to wait in the lawn and went inside, emerging after some time with his wife. She introduced herself as Sunita. One could guess his age by looking at her, and I felt that prosperity had definitely enhanced her attractiveness.

They were amazing hosts. They had both come out only to invite me inside together. The furniture was so white it dazzled the eye. The other guests were already there. Usually, I cannot remember names at the first meeting, but in this case, they came attached with big designations, so they stuck with me: Shriramraghav Singh, chairman of the municipal council; Surendra Pratap Malviya, retired as a gazetted officer, a chemical products scientist, and now running BL(D)U.

'BL(D)U is his dream,' Shalabh said. Here, Malviya-ji interrupted, 'Not just mine. BL(D)U is a dream for all of us. It's a matter of pride for all Noma residents, isn't it?'

A gentleman who sat there thought this introduction was insufficient, so taking matters into his own hands, he added, 'And Dadda is the pride of our town.'

I offered a namaskar to him, and then to everyone. That these folks were the VIPs of this town was apparent not just from their introductions, but from their expressions and manner as well. A tiny hope sprung up in a corner of my mind: Could they perhaps help us in finding Rafique? Big things can often be accomplished with help from unknown quarters after all.

As the introductions went on, Shalabh presented me to everybody as if I were a trophy. The first was Ramjanam Tiwari. 'He lives in London and works as an officer in a very big company.' (Ramjanam told me later that it was Deutsche Bank.) 'He left Noma in 1980 but comes back every year with his family on Janmashtami for the Dol Mela.' Ramjanam's face started to glow by the time Shalabh finished. I felt he would start humming the patriotic song 'Kar chale hum fida' if someone gave him the slightest encouragement. But nobody did. Shalabh pointed towards the front yard;

I couldn't see clearly, but a woman's figure was moving about in the darkness. I was told it was Tiwari-ji's daughter, who worked as a musician at a Yorkshire music academy.

The introductions came to a pause. Surendra Pratap Malviya and Shriramraghav Singh welcomed me formally by placing a shawl around my neck. Ramjanam Tiwari held my hand. He seemed to be perpetually cheerful by nature. With a wide grin on his face he said, 'We will felicitate you in a grand way – "vyapak samman" – at Dadda's premises day after tomorrow.' Everybody applauded. He laughed after saying 'vyapak', looking to the others as if to confirm that he had pronounced the word correctly. Then, settling the matter himself, he said, 'How can I forget Hindi even after becoming an Englishman!'

There were around ten or eleven businessmen who were all involved in some kind of enterprise in town. I wanted to commit to memory all their names, since each held some post in the Mela Committee or in the Mangal Morcha. And there were several who held positions in both. But I couldn't memorize their names just yet, because two most interesting personalities introduced themselves at the same time: Pramod Gupta, who ran a medical store and was the local correspondent for the *Dainik Jagriti*. When I would go to his store later, I'd be greeted by a box labelled 'Your News'. But for now, he introduced himself by reciting a poem.

As if that wasn't enough, Suryabali Upadhyay also introduced himself with a poem. He was the local correspondent for a newspaper called the *Dainik Surya* and ran a coal business. His collection of poetry, *Yeh Sansar Kagaz ki Pudiya*, was to be brought out by a Ghaziabad-based publisher. He told me that eight years before I came to town, Kavi Mahesh had come to Noma and recited his poetry at BL(D)U.

The introductions went on. After listening to everybody, one thing became clear: all of them were in love with themselves. They had several achievements to boast of, but all of them looked restless. It was a relief to get done with them, but then I had to listen to my own introduction. A young man called Amit Jain, who owned a sawmill, ran a school and was the treasurer of the Mangal Morcha, read it out. I felt as if he was talking about someone else. I had forgotten all the things that were being said about me.

While I waited for the introductions to end, a man appeared from nowhere with a bottle of Glenfiddich. But not many people were drinking. It was just me, Shalabh, who sought his wife's permission in an exaggerated manner before touching his glass, and Amit Garg, who came from a family of goldsmiths and had returned to manage the business after studying engineering in Australia.

I was annoyed. I was being made to feel as if I was the only one craving alcohol, that it had been brought out only for my sake, while the rest believed drinking to be sacrilege. The situation would have continued to deteriorate, had that figure from the yard not entered the room. She rolled her lips to toss a silent hello at me, sank into a sofa, and said, 'Constable, one for me too.' The word 'constable' grabbed my attention. I tried to see if it was one of the policemen present at the station this morning.

But it was the woman whom my eye was drawn to more. Her cotton leggings tightly wrapped themselves around her thighs. The drawstring was knotted around her waist like a flower. Her top was the colour of fresh butter, and open from the sides. When she moved around, one could get a glimpse of a crochet bra. She wore an Apple smartwatch on her left hand, and held the glass with two fingers and the thumb of her right, all the while immersed in her phone.

This reminded me that I had not looked at my phone for a while. There were several notifications, but I tapped my message inbox first. There were two texts:

'What's up, my lord? When should I book the return ticket for?'

'Where are you? I've made urad dal for dinner.'

You forget your own habits, you forget the memories that emerge from those habits – but those who remember your habits remember those memories too.

There were also seven missed calls. One was from Anasuya and another from Archana. Five missed calls were from an unknown number. Looking closely, I saw that all five calls were made within a span of five to seven minutes. Truecaller could not tell me anything.

The clock struck ten, but everybody in the gathering continued to drink. It was just the four of us when we began, but by 9 p.m., seven more had joined us, each one supposedly doing so to give me company.

Everyone sat in one group at the start, but after a while, smaller groups were formed. Surrounded by four others, Amit Garg narrated an incident from his student days. Shalabh whispered in my ears, 'He's really laying it on thick.'

Most people surrounded Malviya-ji, or Dadda, which is how he was commonly addressed. He had set a discussion in motion about the importance of image. Thinking I was not participating in the conversation, he pulled me in by asking, 'What do you think about the importance of image in literature?'

'If you're talking about brand image, it is important to create a beautiful image for characters, since it has consequences in the real world,' I answered as per my understanding. 'But if you mean image in myth or fiction, then as a writer, I don't think it is important at all. Especially not in Hindi.'

Dadda acknowledged my words politely and said he was out of touch with contemporary literature. Then he narrated an anecdote: 'When a knowledgeable person once went to Nirala to ask who the greatest Hindi poet of the day was, Nirala replied, "Funny that you should put this question to the greatest Hindi poet himself!"'

'Nobody knows whether this happened or not,' I countered with a laugh. 'And then, even if Nirala did say so, it was reality and not just an image.'

'Can there be a difference between reality and an image?'

'Image or myth comes into use as a word or expression only when there is a difference. Generally, they *are* different. An image has to be constructed.'

Dadda may or may not have found my reply unsavoury, but his followers certainly took great offence. They all tried to teach me a thing or two about image. Dadda also made an attempt. He asked, 'What if a shadow falls upon the image?'

'A shadow can dissipate. Perhaps you mean to say – what if the image gets tainted?'

'Stains can be removed as well,' Dadda shot back. Then, he found a middle path: 'It's possible that self-image has less importance in literature, but the business of life runs on it.' He began to narrate a story about Rolls-Royce.

The young woman had been busy on her phone all this while, but she immediately sat upright upon hearing these words.

'Some hundred years ago, the queen of England sent a Rolls-Royce car as a gift to the king of Tamkuhi. It was an expensive and exquisite gift, and people came from all over just to get a glimpse of it. Forget the vehicle, people would be ecstatic even if they got to touch the tarp that covered it. So many people came to see it that they imposed a fee of one anna as ticket. There is no better car than a Rolls-Royce even now, so imagine the situation back then. You were talking about "brand image" – consider this its origin. What happened next? The car broke down after a week. All attempts were made to fix it. The king and queen had to get on a palanquin from the place where the car had stopped. A mechanic from England was sent for. When the mechanic opened it up, he found there was no engine inside. He was brought in front of the king, who asked him, "I can understand that there is no engine in the car. But what I can't understand is, how did it run for a week?" The mechanic answered, bowing his head low in deference, "The name Rolls-Royce itself was enough, my lord."'

A silence descended upon us all once the story ended. After a while, Dadda added, 'That Raja Sahib was none other than my own late grandfather.'

There is nothing one can say after such 'facts'. Once you wrap a fable around yourself, the fable becomes fact and gets registered as history.

Whatever time I could get to think in the interim, I spent it convincing myself that perhaps it was true that life ran on images. Why squabble over this?

Everybody began to disperse at around 11 p.m. The first to leave was Shyam Kishore Jaiswal, who owned a printing press and was editor of *Agniban*, an evening tabloid. His wife walked over to me and said, 'Do come over to our place as well.' Folding her hands in a namaskar, she said, 'I have not seen any writer before today.' She may have thought it was a nice thing to say, so she repeated it.

Then Malviya-ji – Dadda – departed. He blessed me once again before leaving and said, 'Your presence has graced this town of ours.' He assured me that we would spend more time together at the function day after tomorrow.

There are precious few moments as a writer, and these are far between, when you feel that people adore you.

Others touched Dadda's feet repeatedly right until he got into the car. Amit Jain had taken his leave after touching Dadda's feet, but when he saw that the car door was still open and the vehicle had just started, he raced to touch them once more.

It was decided that I should return to the hotel. Shalabh insisted I stay over, but I excused myself saying I had some work to finish.

❖

Two things happened while I was leaving. First, Sunita handed me one of her paintings as a parting gift. She had signed it at the bottom, with every letter a little drawing in itself.

Then, when I reached the car, Amit Garg came over along with Amit Jain. Both were cordial, and Amit Garg held my hand for a long while. Meanwhile, ten or twelve people gathered around us. It felt to me like the smaller gathering that follows after the dispersal of a big one.

Amit Garg kept repeatedly asking if he could make a request, and I kept saying, 'Yes, of course.'

Finally, he said softly, 'Sir, your Facebook post is bringing disrepute to this town.'

I hadn't looked at my Facebook or Twitter since morning. I had written about coming to Noma, but I wanted to know how exactly it had tarnished the town's image. On the other hand, it was rare for my Facebook posts to get any attention. My lack of popularity was such that I would often 'like' my own posts, and sometimes that would be the only reaction to them. My presence on social media platforms was very limited.

I asked him how my post had brought disrepute to Noma. He remained polite as he replied. Three distinct sentences, one by one, but they all added up to the same thing – that the Dol Mela was just three days away and I was attempting to malign the city at such a time: 'The man has absconded with his student, anyone at the college will tell you about their affair.' 'More than two hundred people have written rubbish about the town because of your post.'

'People are writing nonsense about the Mangal Morcha on Twitter.'

His argument didn't win me over, but it was not right that my actions became a reason to insult someone else. So, I pulled out my phone right there to delete the post. But my phone was old, so the comments on my post appeared very slowly on the screen. Several people had given me their or their friends' phone numbers and said that I could reach out to them at any time.

I was drunk, but not drunk enough to not object to his suggestion that Rafique had 'absconded' with Janaki. I protested, and they immediately apologized, but they remained adamant that Rafique and Janaki had left their homes to live together. I began to worry about how Anasuya would feel if Rafique had really done so. And what if it fell upon me to tell her?

Someone's voice rang out: 'Are you here to look for Rafique?'

This question was akin to asking a guest why he had come. 'What do you think?' I replied in the same manner.

The response to that, however, was hurled at me like a stone, and those present there too felt the pain. 'Everybody is saying you've come to Noma to meet your ex-girlfriend.' The others began to reprimand the person who had asked the question. In the ensuing furore, Shalabh and others came around to the car. I should have answered the question, but I didn't. Why? First, because his own people had pounced upon him. And second, I continued to grapple with his first question.

Thinking aloud, I told myself and the others, 'I haven't come here to *find* Rafique. He is not a lost tune or a memory that needs to be found. He is a living, breathing person, his wife is pregnant, and – now listen to this carefully – not a single person, not one person from this garbage town must have come forward to help her. That's why she thought of me.'

I kept thinking about the voice that had asked me whether I had come to Noma to meet my ex-girlfriend. This meant I was being watched closely, and a false narrative about me was being created and propagated.

I'm not sure if I was asleep or not, but I thought of Anasuya.

Was I thinking of her or imagining her?

If I could, I would have postponed today's sleep to tomorrow and gone to see Anasuya right away. I would have familiarized myself with her situation. I would have asked her in clear terms, 'What do you know about Rafique and Janaki? If you already knew about them, why did you ask me to come?'

But I was exhausted. I somehow reached the hotel. The boy at the reception had fallen asleep. I dragged myself up the stairs. The pages were spread out all over the room to dry, and because the fan would have blown them away,

I went to bed without turning it on. I heard a few pages crinkle under my back and realized that I was only supposed to sleep on the left side of the bed. Just before I fell asleep, I thought of calling Anasuya or Archana. I remembered I had received a call from an unknown number. It was hard to make out anything from the screen, which was worse than blurry. My call was answered right away. 'This is Amandeep speaking. I saw you at the station. I wanted to meet you regarding the matter of Rafique and Janaki.'

'When?'

'Whenever you say. Now?'

How was I to respond? What can one say on the phone anyway? I simply said, 'Tomorrow,' and before I could even hear my own words, I had dozed off.

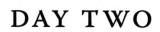

DAY TWO

I woke up to the sound of a bird knocking its beak against the window. Perhaps it wanted to come inside the room. I could have opened the window, but this would have undone the makeshift rope I had made, and the pages of Rafique's diary and notebook were still drying on it. I turned on the bulb, but the light seemed insufficient.

I looked at the phone groggily. There were two messages:

'Talk to me.'

'Have you left?'

I sensed fear, or maybe disbelief, in the second message. The first message was just a call to have a chat.

I replied to the first one: 'Yes, sir.'

It took me a while to reply to the second: 'Still here.'

I remembered the phone call from late last night saying something about Rafique and Janaki. I called that number again. It was answered right away, as if the man was sitting next to his phone.

'This is Amandeep.'

'You were telling me something yesterday. Do you know Rafique and Janaki?'

'I am being watched.'

His mention of 'being watched' shook away any remaining slumber. 'Who is watching you?'

'Not over the phone. Can we meet and talk?'

'Where do we meet? Come to Adarsh Hotel. Or I can come to your house.'

'My house.'

I was annoyed but I also chuckled at the drama unfolding in this tiny town which, in size, couldn't even compete with a Delhi neighbourhood. Or was it that the people here harboured all sorts of fantasies about themselves?

I had a long conversation with Archana. When you live with someone, you speak to them four or five times a day when they're away at work, and this can go on for several years. And yet, here I was, speaking to her after a full twenty-four hours. Hearing her voice, I felt as if she was nearby and would come as soon as I asked her to. I could not see her reaction when I told her about Rafique and Janaki. What I mean is that Archana is someone who usually reacts more through her expressions and not so much through her words. But I couldn't tell from her words whether she believed anything I said or not.

She told me that she spoke with Anasuya after I didn't respond to her call the previous night. 'Anasuya is seven months along. Send for someone from her parents' home or bring her with you to Delhi,' she repeated several times. She also said Anasuya had prepared dinner for me. I told her all about the events of last night, barring the allegation that I had come to Noma to see my ex-girlfriend. I would have told her that too, but it would have been an irritant, especially after the talk of the alleged affair between Rafique and Janaki. When I told her I had a headache, I knew what her next question would be: 'Did you drink?'

'What do you think?' I replied.

I began looking at the pages of the diary while on the phone. Perhaps I could read the ones that were dry. But the air was so humid because of the monsoons that despite lying spread out an entire day and night, the pages had not dried. I did find a couple of damp pages near the window that could be read against the light trickling in from outside:

24/8/15

Jagdish does not like his character. We have performed the play four times, and only now has he come to realize he does not like his character. He wants to break away from us. But why? Because of the mounting pressure from those people. His older brother Suryabali was reluctant to send the report about our performance on 15 August to Dainik Surya. *That news was bound to remain unpublished, and so it did.*

A second page had an entry for 20 June 2015. There were two addresses on it. In the first instance, the name of the addressee had melted away, and only the last lines were visible – 'Flat No. 302, Vikram Marg, Police Lines'. It would be an exaggeration to call the next entry an address. There were simply two words: 'Suhag Studio'.

'I can't understand anything,' I said, expressing my frustration to Archana before cutting the call.

A bus stand lay to the west of Radha Chitra Mandir. That was where the tea stall was to be found. All the shops along the way were closed. Some were in the process of opening up, with water being sprinkled on their yards to be swept, but the dust was not settling. The sun hadn't fully risen in the sky, so the foul smells that engulfed the street during the nights still hung in the air. The tea stall was crowded, with tea of different tastes and kinds being ordered one after another.

I didn't expect Amandeep or anyone else to explain the situation any differently. But a question that had not occurred to me until yesterday now rose up in my mind. What if the news about Rafique and Janaki having an affair was incorrect? How could it be that first a man went missing, then a young woman disappeared, and yet barely anybody knew about it in such a small and peaceful town? I couldn't think beyond this. I couldn't think about what would happen even if people were aware about Rafique and Janaki's disappearance. What then? Does the system allow us to participate in the grief of others by offering them legal help? Can we fight institutions on behalf of our friends with the same conviction as we do for our family?

Let's assume that I went missing one day – the thought itself terrified me. What if I actually went missing? What would Archana do? But how could I disappear unless someone deliberately made me disappear? How was Rafique's mental health? Did he talk to himself? If he did, since when had he done so? And even if he didn't, it was important to know his mental state. From what I had read so far, his diary was not some glorious outpouring of emotions, so it seemed unlikely that I'd find any clues there.

A signboard for 'Furkan Vastralaya' hung right across from the tea stall. The clothes shop was closed, but the name stayed on in my mind because the papers Anasuya had handed me were in a plastic bag from this very store.

I wanted to reconstruct an entire sequence of events in my mind that I had not witnessed at all. Had Rafique and Anasuya visited this shop? What time was it? Had the dust settled, or did it fly all around? What did they buy? How did a plastic bag from this shop enter their lives after all?

By the time the sun was up in the sky, I had already gulped down three cups of tea.

When I got poori-sabzi packed for Anasuya and me, I had absolutely no idea that I would find Kushalpal, Mukesh, Jagdish and a fourth, Neeraj, at her place. I was astonished by the support Anasuya received through their continued presence and assistance. Were Rafique's students really so attached to him? Without wasting a moment, I sent Kushal to fetch breakfast for everyone.

The morning sunlight came down into her balcony as if it had slipped and fallen there. It remained in one spot, not moving an inch. All of us stood under its canopy except Anasuya. She sat on a chair with broken arms, wearing a polka-dotted maxi dress and a longish dupatta that covered her belly. She had wrapped another dupatta around her ears and throat. Her face was taut and glowing.

Everybody was drinking their tea silently. When I realized that the sun would not leave us alone, I talked about the previous night, telling them everything, even the Rolls-Royce story. As I spoke, I remembered other things that had been lost during the gathering. I told Anasuya that Archana had invited her to Delhi, and that the daroga had said he would soon find Rafique.

Kushal had not returned with breakfast yet, and I tried calling him. The opening lines of Ellie Goulding's song 'Love me like you do...' played as the caller tune on his phone, which ended with the line, 'I will let you set the pace.' This town continued to baffle me. For the first time ever, I was hearing this song as someone's caller tune.

We then decided Anasuya would eat the pooris while the rest of us would go over to the shop. Then, we were to visit Janaki's village.

Every time Kushal's companions called him, I asked them to put the phone on speaker so that I could listen to the song until the end. They called him several times before we reached Janaki's village, so we heard the song several times too.

I WOULD TURN THIRTY-THREE IN A few months, but this was the first time I was visiting a village. Whenever I wrote a short story in which a village figured, I would rely on facts I had read in books and other stories, I would recall movies, talk to numerous people who came from villages and, most importantly, to those who still remained in touch with their villages and visited regularly.

Janaki's village, called Sujja, had mostly Brahmins with the surname Dubey living in it. A left turn three kilometres after Noma towards Lar Road would lead you to a semi-pucca road that cut right through Sujja, and there onwards to Bhagalpur. The three students, who sat in the back, expressed their regret at not knowing the address of a girl who not only studied with them in the same college but was also part of their theatre group. But we didn't have to ask around too much. We stopped near a man holding a lathi and wearing a loincloth, who looked like a shepherd. Before I could say anything, he asked, 'You want to go to Ramkripal Dubey's house?'

We said no. Then he asked again, 'Arey, the house of the girl who has gone missing, no?'

This time, we said yes.

He patiently gave us the directions.

A police jeep was already parked outside the house.

There was silence all around.

This was an entirely different world.

Despite such terrible circumstances, the family still remained hospitable. Wooden stools had been placed on the veranda. No sooner had we taken our seats than two young men emerged from inside with a jug full of water, clean steel tumblers, and a tray filled with light-yellow laddus.

We met Janaki's father, Ramkripal Dubey. Mukesh introduced us to him. Ramkripal told us that three constables had been going through Rukkhi's room over and over for the last couple of hours. Janaki was addressed as 'Rukkhi' at home – another name for a squirrel. The pet name spoke volumes about how much they loved their daughter. Ramkripal told us a lot of things. How he regretted that, despite Rukkhi getting a seat in Gorakhpur University, he could not let her study away from home. He didn't have much money and was already paying for Rukkhi's brother Roshan's engineering degree, which was why Gorakhpur was beyond his means.

Ramkripal kept talking incessantly in a low voice. Perhaps he thought his daughter might be hidden somewhere within his words and talking to us could allow him to reach her.

A thought nagged at me – had someone informed the police about our decision to come here? Today was the fourth day that Janaki had been missing, and the police had arrived only now. So, my apprehension seemed justified. But then I laughed – how on earth could we, with all our limitations, have scared the police into doing its work?

When I asked for Ramkripal's phone number, he took me aside. 'Are you a journalist?' he asked. His question was filled with intense hope. He told me that on the day Rukkhi had not come home, his son, with the help of a friend, had put him in touch with a journalist. 'He asked me everything over a phone call and requested her photo over WhatsApp. The news item was published in *Dainik Jagriti* too, but he has not answered our call since then.'

I said, 'I am not a journalist. I am Rafique's friend. I've come from Delhi.'

Something stirred in him when I mentioned Rafique. His eyes glinted. 'We heard the news of his disappearance. He came to our home twice. He was Rukkhi's teacher and also ran a theatre group. I was not in favour of it, but I never stopped her from participating in those activities. Not once did I stop her. Never.'

As if the momentum of his speech was beginning to fade, he looked up and shook his head in denial for a while.

A small boy, who looked to be around eight or nine, came and stood by Ramkripal's side and spoke to him in Bhojpuri: '*Ye lo ke bhittar bolawal ja ta.*' They're being called inside. Besides a few instances in films and on the streets of Delhi, this was my first encounter with the Bhojpuri language.

The boy led us indoors. As I was about to follow him, Ramkripal put a hand on my shoulder and said, 'Please make Rukkhi's mother understand.'

'Sure,' I said. Both she and I needed to understand what was happening.

We went from the veranda into a small room. A courtyard lay beyond, past another door in a straight line from the one we had entered by. As I stepped into the courtyard, I saw several women sitting on a tarpaulin. One sat with her back against a wall, seemingly not in her senses. She saw me come in, and I could see her eyes welling up with tears when I looked at her. Perhaps she couldn't stand the fact that a stranger had seen her helplessness and despair so closely.

The other women had been sitting as if at a wake. They gathered themselves when they saw us five men walk in. One wanted to bring chairs from outside, but I insisted it was not necessary. All of us sat on the tarp with the women.

I presumed the room on the right which the constables were going through must belong to Janaki. I didn't like the sight of a room filled with policemen, so I looked around for other signs that it was Janaki's room. I saw the iconic photograph of the poet Muktibodh hanging right above the door. He stood to the right in the picture, holding a burning matchstick to a beedi, and his gesture was so lively that it felt like the beedi would light up any second now. A few lines from one of his poems were scribbled with a black pen to the left:

Consider it ego or
A superiority complex
Or something similar
But the truth is that
We don't have the time
To achieve
So-called success in life,
We are not idle!
We are extremely busy.

The courtyard had a narrow scaffolding, and it seemed as if the rain had tried getting rid of the last line of the verse. But the line remained – 'We are extremely busy.' Something was written on the right edge of the picture, where the frame ended. A two-letter name, written in such a tiny scrawl that it was impossible to read. The second letter was drawn as a brush.

There was a green-coloured handpump in the courtyard with a worn-out handle. A few unwashed utensils lay beside it. A Singer sewing machine was on the other side of the courtyard, and several clothes had been dumped on it. A book was visible in the pile, and the cover looked familiar. Greyish-white, or rather, off-white. The silence was too much to endure, so I got up to check the book out.

'Oh my god!' The words escaped my mouth before I knew it, and then, 'Who reads this?' I already knew the answer, but I said it aloud in my excitement.

'Rukkhi Di,' a girl replied.

'Are you her sister?'

'Yes.'

'May I see a picture of her?'

The book was the second volume of Mayakovsky's poetry, an old text published by Raduga Publications, a state-owned publisher in the Soviet Union. You couldn't find it in shops any more. I had both volumes at home, but I had never read either. Raduga had collected Mayakovsky's long poems in the second volume. There was a rough sketch of the poet on the endpaper in front. Below it was a signature: 'Rafique Neel'. All I could think of at that moment was that here was a man who had dedicated himself to educating a new generation. Jagdish and Mukesh walked over. Jagdish kept quiet as Mukesh said, 'Rafique Sir used to assign us a book every month. Mayakovsky's first volume was assigned to me. On the last Monday of the month, the day when Noma's market is shut, we were supposed to get together and speak about the book, or poem, or whatever the work was. This month, Kushal got the most difficult book.' He did not mention the name of the book but chuckled instead. An innocent chuckle.

'Not *used to* assign a book, *assigns* a book,' I whispered in his ear.

One of the policemen came outside upon hearing us. It was the third constable from the previous day. He was either pleased to see me or did a great job pretending to be, because he greeted me effusively. Then he took the book from my hands and said, 'We're conducting a search.' I remembered nothing else except the indignity of the previous day, so I said to him as he walked away, 'It's a book of poems.' Without turning around, he acknowledged me with a grunt.

Janaki's sister introduced herself as Maithili and handed me a bundle of eight or ten photos. There was a radiance on Janaki's face in these pictures that was missing from the image printed in the newspaper.

Maithili requested us to have lunch with them. We looked at our watches; it was already quarter past one.

I had wanted to talk to Janaki's mother, but I could not even bring myself to look her in the eye. I did not know her, but I could very well understand what she was going through. Because I could empathize with her, I wanted to say something, but the words just wouldn't come out of my mouth. She did not know us either but looked at us again and again. Unlike Janaki's father, she was speechless. Her stony eyes did all the talking. It seemed as if her tears had dried up, but I was never right about these things.

As I hadn't said anything, I tried to touch her feet before leaving. But ... Oh, how can I explain the 'but', especially when I had to face a mother. She threw herself at my feet instead. And those cries! I can never forget those cries.

As she bowed, she struck her head so hard I could hear the
sound it made upon hitting the floor. If I hadn't withdrawn
my feet in embarrassment, perhaps the blow would have
hurt her less. But her pain was not just physical. Her cries
broke past her dammed emotions. Addressing me – yes,
me! – she wailed, '*Hamri bahini key khoji da, ae babu.
Hamri bahini ke bola da.*' Help us find our daughter, sir.
Bring her back.

Everyone in the courtyard began to weep after that.
Jagdish and Neeraj cried into each other's shoulders.
Mukesh wept over a wall. The women covered their eyes
with the ends of their saris. A crying Maithili tried to
console her howling mother. I wanted to console everyone,
but my throat was choked with emotions.

Our collective cries united us as one.

The teardrops that fell in Janaki's courtyard chased us in the
car as well. The car moved at great speed – without a care
for the poor condition of the road and the potholes. Sahadeo
looked straight ahead and did not pay attention to anything
else, as if he wanted to run over the 'system'. He dropped
us off at Radha Chitra Mandir. The place was buzzing with
people since the noon show of *Bajrangi Bhaijaan* had just
ended, and the matinee show was about to begin.

I WAS BY MYSELF FOR THE first time since the morning, but this lasted only until the time I entered the police station. I like to be alone after being around others for an extended period of time, and when I cannot, I turn irritable and lash out. I had wanted to ask Sahadeo to drop us directly at the station, but the past two hours had been so unbearably rough on us all that we felt like accomplices in a horrible crime and could not bring ourselves to say anything.

I was relieved to see Shalabh. I waited for about five or six minutes after sending him a message, and then he came to fetch me. He said he was just about to call me. 'What are you up to in the evening?' he asked.

'I feel like being alone today.'

'Let's plan for tomorrow evening then.'

The conversation continued as we went to his office, which was a small one but tastefully decorated. A handful of files lay on the desk. There were other objects too that were legally necessary. Our beloved tricolour, of course. It had a sticker on its base that had become discoloured, probably as the result of attempting to remove it. Gandhi's picture was on the back wall.

'I was just about to give you a call,' he said again.

'Yes.'

I told him someone called Amandeep had called, and how he wanted to tell me something about Rafique and Janaki but was too scared. Shalabh let out a loud guffaw. He leaned back in his chair as if he had an easy explanation to offer. 'So he reached out to you as well! The man wants to be the centre of attention. He sat in this chair before me, and is suspended at the moment.' When I did not react to this, he reiterated. 'Suspended! A matter of financial misappropriation has come to light.'

'Why did the matter come out now?' I asked curiously.

'How can I say why now?' The question perturbed him. 'Only the constable who was complicit in this sin and whose conscience has woken up now can give us an answer. Amandeep was posted at Baitalpur station at the time and was about to get promoted.'

Both of us stayed quiet for a while. There was no sound at all. Then Shalabh picked up the conversation again, 'Even a writer like you will be surprised to hear the constable's account.'

I was surprised anyway. Was 'financial misappropriation' enough reason to suspend police officials now!

'But why does Amandeep want to contact me? I couldn't sense any deceit in his voice.'

'Perhaps he wants your help in getting reinstated. Help him if you can. You know people at the top. There is no need otherwise to pay attention to his ludicrous gossip. But do let me know if he tries to get in touch again.' He paused momentarily. 'Rafique's matter, on the other hand, seems to be taking a different turn. This is not a simple matter of disappearance or abduction, as everyone has been thinking. Perhaps you too were thinking along the same lines as your friend. Did you all visit Janaki's place?'

I was stunned. 'Have you put us under surveillance?'

'No, boss. One of the constables who went there told me. Our investigations suggest this is a matter of a romantic relationship. But the meticulous way in which it was planned also indicates something beyond a simple love affair, so we're investigating that angle too.' He pulled his phone out, the latest iPhone. Opening WhatsApp, he tapped on a number and played a video for me.

The video was shot haphazardly. The entire frame was shaking as if the camera was not still. One could see Rafique lying down. I recognized Rafique, but Shalabh still said, 'This is your friend, or your friend's shauhar, whatever you want to call him.'

Rafique was lying down on a culvert by the roadside. The camera moved to the right, and a young lady appeared. It was clear that this was Janaki. Her gait was unusual, which was noticed by the person behind the camera too, for the lens panned down to her feet for a couple of seconds before returning to her face. Now both of them appeared in the frame. Rafique had left just enough space on the side of the culvert for Janaki to sit.

Rafique: You've come?

Janaki: So it would seem.

They both went silent. Then they looked upwards in the same direction. Their gaze was so steady that it became imprinted on my mind.

Janaki: My uncle is in the market today. He had called.

Rafique: Say, we have to leave now.

Janaki: Understand, we have to leave now.

Rafique: Understood, we have to leave now.

Janaki: Must you stand atop your pedestal and ridicule others all the time, Neju? Is this what your Allah-Allah-Khair-Salla has taught you?

Rafique: He has also taught me that people should not be late, but they are.

Janaki: Stop it.

Rafique: Stopped it … Rakesh and Supriya went to the lodge.

Janaki: Find someone else you can go to a lodge with.

The video ended here. Shalabh looked at me for a while, then said, 'How will you tell your friend?'

After recovering from the shock of the video, I requested him to send it to me. But he said sharing police evidence was not legally allowed. Instead, he handed his phone over to me. 'You may watch it on this.' Which I did, several times over.

I pondered over what my reaction to the video should be. Questions erupted in my mind: Who shot it? If a man and a woman are in a relationship and not performing an act, would they allow someone to shoot such a video? For all I knew, it could very well be a scene from one of their street plays. One or two people were visible in the background too. And why did Janaki address Rafique as 'Neju'?

Shalabh had two answers for all my questions. The first – his answer to my last question – was terribly unconvincing. 'Perhaps someone else has laid claim to the name "Rafique", like his wife. Which is why she wanted to give him her own special name.' As for the other questions, he merely sighed and said, 'So you're a video specialist too? And have you seen this video before? Is that why you have an explanation ready?' This last was intended as a warning for me to not overstep my bounds.

Then he changed the topic and said, 'The member of Parliament, Madam Khudaija Bibi Lari, called again. She said we had to take good care of you. How do you know her?' Then he added, as if he suddenly thought his question was incomplete, 'I mean, does she know you through your books or is there a family connection?'

I was hearing her name for the first time. I silently thanked the owner of my publishing house and told Shalabh, 'It's her grace, that's all. Otherwise, who am I that she should know me?'

'Not at all! Who doesn't respect writers?' He seemed hellbent on pursuing this subject.

I thought I should ask him if he did too, but there were other important questions, so I let it go. 'But you can't reach a conclusion on the basis of this video, can you?'

'We are looking for other evidence too.'

'This has to be a video from a performance of their street play.'

'You are saying this for the sake of your friend.'

'Not for the sake of my friend, but for the sake of justice!'

'We are always there for the sake of justice,' he said and pointed towards the motto of the state police. 'We suspended one of ours for the sake of justice. Don't you think that's proof enough?'

All the time I was at the station, the question of how to tell Anasuya what I had learnt continued to bother me. What would she go through? What more must she go through? When I tell her, will she look at me? What will she think about Rafique? Will she remember the moments when she might have had doubts about Rafique and Janaki and brushed them aside? Was it even necessary to give this information to a pregnant woman? You could search for a person who had gone against their will. But to look for someone who had left of their own volition would be like an act of revenge. That person should be let go. Those who want to leave must be allowed to leave. Love should not have any dilemmas.

But is it really so easy? How can you let go of someone you love? Perhaps you could let a lover leave; in fact, you should let them go. But what about someone you were married to? Should you go looking for them for the sake of the child in your womb?

I wanted to go to Anasuya, but I didn't want to tell her anything. This dilemma would have killed me, had she not called and said she was on her way to the hospital. I was disheartened that she hadn't told me earlier. I would have gone along myself, or sent Sahadeo with her, or made better arrangements.

'How are you going?' I asked her.

She replied as if there was nothing unusual about her answer. If I hadn't read that page from Rafique's diary, I would have found it very unusual.

I was exhausted. If it was any other day, I would have gone off to sleep. I could sleep whenever I wanted, which was a blessing. And I really wanted to sleep at that moment, but the thought of Anasuya would not leave my mind. The diary's pages had still not dried. After watching the video, I had lost interest in reading his diary, but Rafique's writing pulled me back towards it like a magnet. Most of the papers strewn across the room were as damp as before, but those spread out in the bathroom were less so. Some had even dried completely. I read these until I fell asleep.

6/4/15

Madam Anasuya wants to give me a surprise. I hope that when she gives me the surprise, my expressions also convey that it is indeed a surprise to me. The landlord's wife has asked me not to tell Anasuya that she has already told me. But madam, you should have taken me with you to the doctor. I wanted to experience the joy of discovering you were going to become a mother together with you.

The undergraduate examinations begin tomorrow. I have to be the invigilator every day. To be an invigilator is also like playing a character.

12/8/15
The landlord does not like our theatre group's office. But brother, we've just rented one room. He came over and sat in on the rehearsal. If his name was Motumal, it wouldn't have been out of place – just like that children's rhyme, 'The fat man sat on the chair / The chair cried out in despair.' It was only from the chair's creaking that we realized someone else was in the office too. He began to say that the play wouldn't be allowed to go on. The neighbours were apparently objecting to it. All I had to offer him was a role. I thought of offering him Amit's role, but he absolutely didn't want it. I wasn't upset. When people aren't upset by crimes and murders but get infuriated by discussions around them, what's the point of feeling bad about this? My students, who are turning into my friends, my companions, consider this my cowardice. But if I don't mind what Motumal has to say, why should I feel bad about what these rookies say?

I addressed my companions in a bid to make him listen: Are you people also afraid of Junior Dadda?

We have to stop going there from tomorrow. Motumal has confiscated our things. Kushal managed to rescue his uniform and Mukesh his turban.

The landlord said that if any wear and tear had taken place in the room, he would cover the expenses by selling our stuff.

Where will we do the rehearsals from tomorrow?

If I ask Anasuya, she will say, 'Do it at home.' But I won't. She doesn't like noise.

So then, dear Rafique, where will you do the rehearsals from tomorrow?

How will you perform on 15 August?

DAY THREE

DAY THREE

This MORNING TOO BEGAN AT the tea stall near the bus stand. What was different was that I had arrived fairly early today, so there was almost no one there. I had been mulling over a problem since the morning. The things I could not tell Anasuya the previous night weighed me down. And all that weight on my mind did not let me see how drastic a turn things had taken. In fact, it was Anasuya who would tell me about this.

I would have felt better if Archana had accompanied me. The ritual of installing the kalash – the vessel – for the Dol Mela was to be held at Dadda's home today. This was an important event, and I had been invited as well. But the matter of Rafique and Janaki was disturbing me so much that I decided to go to Anasuya's place first. An old woman was there to see her. It was Jagdish's mother.

I told Anasuya everything I had learnt the previous day, but I could not tell her why Rafique might have decided to leave home. Gathering some courage, I finally asked her, 'Did Rafique ever mention Janaki? Do you remember anything?'

'Yes. He always mentions her name. She is his student.'

'People are saying all sorts of things about the two of them.'

When I said that, she stood up and walked across the room to go outside. She returned holding the day's paper and opened it to the third page. On the top right was an article that read: 'Author Arjun Kumar to be felicitated at BL(D)U.' A description of the function followed. The news also mentioned that a symposium had been organized.

Below this was another news item: 'Love Jihad: Muslim teacher absconds with Hindu student.'

'Love' was printed in red and 'Jihad' in green. The piece was pretty long. 'A matter of love jihad' was printed in bold. I feared for Anasuya's safety as soon as I saw it. The intriguing bit about the report was that it had very little information about the meetings between Rafique and Janaki. Such reports generally carried information such as the number of years the couple knew each other, whether they had been seen together earlier, what a neighbour had said, and what the wife had said. But there was nothing of this sort. What was dwelt on in detail, however, was that Rafique's current wife was also a Hindu, and his modus operandi suggested that he was part of a gang. It was lamented that he had decided to leave his wife while she was pregnant. The article also said that Janaki's family had severed relations with her. Anasuya was mentioned at the end: 'His wife refused to comment on the situation.'

Anasuya said this was a lie. 'Nobody bothered to ask me anything.'

'You have to come to Delhi with me.'

'This report is a lie.'

'It's published in the paper now.'

'I am worried about Rafique. If this news were true, the police would have certainly registered a report. Rafique isn't like this.'

'I am afraid for you. People can harm you using Janaki as an excuse. Think about your unborn child. Come with me to Delhi. You can return after everything has settled down.'

'Return to whom?'

I had no answer to this question, merely arguments that would make my life easier but not another's. I wondered whether Anasuya's repeated denials of the news report came from a place of feeling abandoned rather than from her trust in Rafique. Lies and betrayals are often tolerated in relationships because people don't want to be left alone. They brush aside all red flags and cover naked truths with their own delusions. But those who are aware that they have no control over love, they don't fall into the trap of truth, lies and betrayals.

This meeting was bound to end somewhere, so I repeated, a little loudly this time, 'Archana has invited you. Come to Delhi. Think about your unborn child.'

She sat right there on a stool. Why did I not have anything else to say to her? I wanted to talk about the weather, but it would have been pointless in these circumstances. Talking about her brothers would have been equally futile. Rafique's absence had filled up all the space around us to such an extent that there was no room for words.

❖

She walked down the stairs to see me off. 'There's a literary function in the afternoon,' I told her while standing in the sun on the stairs. 'I will return in the evening. You are coming along with me.' I was now very close to her and was looking up at her from a step below – an inverse of the photograph that had been found in my house.

A bicycle was parked downstairs near the door. Waiting for its rider. Anasuya, who had been calm and composed so far, grabbed its handle and seat and began to weep, her head bowed. She repeated between her sobs, 'This is all a lie, a lie, all a lie.' Those who passed by may have thought I was part of the scene, but only I knew that I was no more than a bystander.

To comfort her, I placed a hand on her shoulder. On a spot that was at the very edge of her shoulder, beyond which the body didn't exist and only memory or imagination did. 'Stop crying. Please, stop crying. Be brave. Think of your unborn child.' I found myself using the unborn child as my weapon. I was seized by the thought that if I, who had only been around for a day or so, was using a child against a woman or her emotions, how terribly and repeatedly must those who live together use the same weapon all their lives. Mankind left no stone unturned in transforming this natural gift of a woman into a curse.

The touch of her shoulder birthed a desire within me. I wished I could enter her skin through this timid touch. I wished it were possible for us to switch skins. Then her sorrows would become mine, and the advantage I had of being able to observe her troubles from a distance would become hers. But alas! If it were so, I could also have found out what hurt her more – that Rafique wasn't around, or that he had betrayed her. I wanted to peer into her soul and learn what her answer would be if Rafique told her he didn't want to be with her any more, that he wanted to be with Janaki. I would have felt the movements of her child. But touch has its limitations – it doesn't transform.

'Is this Rafique's cycle?'

She grunted in affirmation, the way one says 'yes' with a closed mouth using one's breath.

'I am taking it. I will bring it back when I return in the evening to pick you up...' I stressed on the 'pick you up'. Then I repeated myself because I wanted to hear her say yes.

But she wasn't going to say yes, and she did not.

I decided to take a ride around town, but the bicycle was in bad shape. Deep grooves had formed on the handlebars where Rafique's fingers might have held them, and I was having a hard time settling my own fingers on them properly. If someone recognized Rafique's cycle, they might have been confused. The cycle did have brakes, but they didn't really work. One had to use one's feet to make it come to a halt.

The road was narrow. I turned east from the market, mindful that if I went around in a circle, I would reach the police station on the west. The town ended after about a kilometre to the east, but the road went on. There were fewer people here. A school called Saraswati Shishu Evam

Bal Vidya Mandir marked the town's limits. No one was outside, so I guessed classes might have been on. Riding further ahead, I hit a crossroads. I had to choose a path and I turned right. The road to the left must have led to Bihar via Mehrauna.

I almost ran into a truck near the Durga temple on the Noma crossroads. The government hospital was a little ahead. This is where the journalist Pramod Gupta had his medicine shop. I didn't have any trouble finding it: Navbharat Medical Store, directly opposite the hospital. The signboard displayed the names of the two newspapers Gupta wrote for. Beneath it was a board attesting to his membership at a human rights organization.

He rose from his seat when he saw me getting off the bicycle. There were two or three customers at his shop. 'You have a cure for every disease, it seems,' I said, pointing to the signboards that announced his interest in medicine, journalism and human rights. 'Arey, maharaj,' he took my hand and welcomed me with extreme humility. When he asked about the cycle, it occurred to me that it must have been him who had filed the report about Rafique and Janaki. I had no objection to his report. But I wanted to know how he could write that Rafique's wife had refused to say anything when he hadn't spoken to Anasuya at all.

He gave his reason, and what a reason it was: 'Even if I had asked her, would she have been able to say anything? I have accorded her some honour at least. Believe me, sir, it is indeed a matter of love jihad.'

'Don't call me sir, please.'

'As you wish, sir!' This time, the 'sir' was accompanied by a loud guffaw. 'Which story will you read at the function?'

'There was no talk of reading a story. Do I have to?'

'What are you saying, sir! It would be lovely to listen to one of your love stories. This is what the programme should be, and indeed will be.'

I brought the conversation back to my point. 'But how can you say this is love jihad? Where is the evidence? Did the police ask you to do so? People can hurt Anasuya because of your report.'

'The thing is, sir-ji, the woman should also have thought about all this. She should have thought about all this before getting into a love marriage. There was always going to be some danger...'

'What sort of talk is this?'

'Sir, rest assured, nothing will happen,' he softened at my objection.

This was said in the same way that Shalabh had told me they would find Rafique. But I no longer felt the same kind of reassurance I had felt then.

We took each other's leave promising to meet again at the function, but not before he made me drink two cups of tea. He said that it was the house rule – a visitor could depart only after drinking two cups.

I felt like going to the police station but wasn't sure if I would find Shalabh there. I wanted to know how Rafique, who had been a 'missing person' until the party two nights ago – where I was asked to remove my Facebook post about him – had turned into a 'love jihadi' in this morning's newspaper. The news report had probably been written and edited, and its placement on the third page fixed as well, while Shalabh had been assuring me he would find Rafique. He must have kept it from me.

A young Sikh man sat on the bench near the reception. The two of us looked at each other. As I started climbing the stairs, the boy at the reception told me that this gentleman had been waiting for me. By the time he said this, I had already climbed half the stairs, so I turned around to look at the man once more. I recalled he was the same man who had exchanged pleasantries with Rafique's students at the police station, and Kushalpal had even gone up to chat with him. He followed me to my room.

'My name is Amandeep Singh. I was an assistant sub-inspector here until a month and a half ago,' he said.

I remembered he had called me the previous night to say something about Rafique and Janaki. Hearing his name, I looked towards the door. I couldn't see properly whether it was locked or not, so I got up to check. It was locked.

He spoke slowly, trying to conceal his anxiety, pausing after every word: 'Perhaps you didn't want to see me.'

'You hadn't given me your address. How did you get my phone number? And are you suspended right now?'

'Yes, I'm suspended. But my suspension doesn't disprove my point that this is not a matter of love jihad.'

'Please tell me if you have evidence to the contrary. The police have a video in their possession.'

'Do you trust their stories? Nobody understands their plan, but since everybody is scared, they are supporting them. Rafique wanted to disseminate his mania, a mania which he called a "message", to thousands through multiple performances of his street play during the Dol Mela. Now these people will use that same festival to spread *their* message.'

'Who are these people?'

'The same ones who are felicitating you.'

'What rubbish!'

'The Mangal Morcha.'

'Hold on, sir-ji, hold on,' I shouted him down. His explanation sounded like a cooked-up story. The situation was not so bad that I had to start believing a suspended police officer's theory. But how do you shoo away a man who has barged into your hotel room?

'Sir, the truth is being hidden behind a huge veil. You have also been used as a tool. Weren't you asked to remove your Facebook post?'

'Is this all the evidence you have?' The derision in my voice was, in fact, borne out of belief. Very few realities are as clear as death, and most truths turn hazy under a shroud of lies. But the moment you clear away a layer of the haze, reality peeks out. I was more than ready to admit this was not a matter of love jihad – but for Anasuya's sake, not mine, since that was what she too claimed. But the media, the police, the city, the system – all of them could not possibly be fabricating the truth.

He stood right in front of me. He had gone silent – perhaps because I had derided him – and now looked at the papers strewn all over the room. I didn't like the way he looked around. I feared I was being followed under the pretext of searching for Rafique's diary and notes.

To help him become more comfortable and get past my earlier tone, I offered him tea. I even asked him if he needed help dealing with the matter of his suspension. He chuckled at first, then said he was in a hurry. He mentioned he was under surveillance, and added that the video clip of Rafique and Janaki that was being presented as evidence by the police was from a rehearsal of one of their plays.

He came up close to me as he said this. His fear was evident now. I asked him to sit, but he repeated that he was in a hurry. He said I was also being followed.

Then he gave me a new name – Niyaz. 'I had saved him from getting lynched by a mob. You should meet him. If he is around, you will find him at Suhag Studio.' He held a piece of yellow paper in his hand. It had a phone number on one side and directions to Suhag Studio from Radha Chitra Mandir on the other.

I faintly recalled that I had read about Suhag Studio on a dry page from Rafique's diary, but at that moment, all of it seemed to be a figment of the suspended daroga's imagination. I felt like laughing, and the feeling would have stayed had he not told me something baffling before leaving. He added that he had actually come to just tell me this:

'Kushalpal has also gone missing since yesterday afternoon.'

Kushalpal!

Nobody had heard from him since he had left to fetch pooris the other day. Of Rafique's three students, Kushal was the tallest and strongest, and always took the lead in speaking to others. He might have been the same size as Amandeep, the suspended policeman. The steadfastness with which these guys stood by Anasuya was exemplary. I had thought of having a long conversation with them when they left the hotel the day before. I wanted to get to know these brave young men better, but now I was being told Kushal had also not come back home. I had Mukesh's phone number. He had sent me a few photos and videos that I had not been able to download.

When I called Mukesh, his phone was answered by a woman. She seemed quite disinterested in the conversation. 'There is too much noise, speak louder,' she kept repeating. 'Can you give it to Mukesh?' I asked over and over then eventually hung up, hoping that she would ask him to call back.

The phone rang suddenly, like a flash of memory. Both sadness and anger washed over me when I saw who it was. Anger, because I didn't know why I was so afraid. Of what or whom? And sadness, over the fact that I was being used.

It was Archana.

I HAD TO VISIT SUHAG STUDIO. I had to look for Niyaz. But before I did so, I decided to read a few pages of the disorderly, dried-up bunch from Rafique's diary.

The date was listed as 28 June 2015. It looked like a list of characters in a play. A name was written in the left column, and another on the right. Eight lines in all. It was difficult to figure out which names belonged to the characters, and which to the actors. Amandeep's name was on top, and Kushalpal's name was listed next to it. Below Amandeep, there was Niyaz. On its right was Rafique. I understood then that the left column listed out the characters, while the actors' names were on the right. In between was a line that joined the two names, as thin as the margin between dusk and night:

Amandeep .... Kushalpal
Niyaz .... Rafique
Mangal .... Jagdish
Amangal .... Mukesh
Anuradha .... Whom to choose? (Janaki**)
Chaiwallah .... Neeraj

> *Person one* .... *Who?*
> *Person two* .... *Who?*

The title of this script or play was listed below: *Bachane Wala Hai Bhagwan!* – The One Who Saves Is God! From here on, the page had completely dissolved, to the extent that even 'Bhagwan' was my own guess; the discoloured page only said, *'Bachane Wala Hai Bhag'*. I added the letters and the exclamation mark as per my own understanding.

It dawned on me that this list would have been prepared in the presence of others. The handwriting was the same as on the other pages, so it wouldn't be correct to say someone else had prepared the list. But the way 'Rafique' was listed across from 'Niyaz', it was plausible that other people were around and that there may have been a discussion about it. If Rafique had written it by himself, or if I were Rafique and had written this in inexplicable solitude, I would have perhaps jotted down 'me' in the first person instead of writing my own name.

I didn't like the play's title. For the past two days, my mind had been sculpting an image of Rafique through his diary, his lively literary engagements and his students. All of it, however, began to crumble because of the title. His accomplishments at the ground level with his students had fortified his image as a man of hard work and perseverance in my mind. Such a perception was natural. I knew little about him, but the fact that he was Anasuya's husband, and not one bought with dowry but earned with love – a fact that, even by itself, created a good impression. I respected him even more because of the struggles that came his way because of the marriage. As I grew older, I had begun to believe that 'love marriage' was not made for Indian society. One couldn't cut oneself off from society for the sake of a woman. One could not leave everything for love. But whenever I heard of a love marriage, a certain kind of respect took root in my heart for such couples.

Rafique's image actually began to crumble because of the hope that had arisen when I saw the cast of the play. I had thought I was going to get a glimpse into the behind-the-scenes moments of the production of a world-renowned play. I had started wondering which play it could be even before I saw the cast. I was thrilled to peek into the diary of a dynamic young theatre director in a mofussil town of less than 25,000 people. What play could it be? I thought of several names: *Melancholia*? *The Girl on the Sofa*? *Piano for Sale*? *The Caucasian Chalk Circle*? *Charandas Chor*? Which one would it be?

But the title – *Bachane Wala Hai Bhagwan!* – felt as if the play had been created for an ad agency or as part of a marketing campaign. Was it for the same agency that Rafique had mentioned on a previous page as one that owed him money? When I tried to turn to that page, it came apart. I tried to recall the name of the agency. Was it M.K. or R.K.?

Most pages of the diary and notebooks were still damp. I tried to determine what the play was about, or its story, from the few dried pages. Then it occurred to me that rather than getting entangled in the play, I needed to browse the pages to look for clues into Rafique's disappearance.

Seeing Janaki's association with the play here, I began to regret all that I had thought so far about her. From the very beginning, whenever one spoke of Janaki – the newspaper report that carried the news about her disappearance, the inspector's mention of her, and now the report about love jihad – my scepticism had repeatedly hinted that the truth lay somewhere in the primeval connection between man and woman. When that thought first came to me, I refuted it almost immediately. I had no right to think like this about others. If there was a relationship between the two – if it ever existed or even if it did not – it was not my business, nor was it ethical to suspect them. But when the daroga too said it, it seemed as if all signs were indeed pointing at a relationship between them. Also, if such a relationship did exist, nobody would write about it in their diary.

What I should have done, in fact, was ask Kushal, Jagdish, or some other students about them. But Kushal was not around any more for me to ask. Mukesh was yet to call me back, and I did not have Jagdish's number. I could now only ask Anasuya. I sent her a message instead of calling: 'Jagdish's phone number?'

There was a knock on the door.

There wasn't enough light in the room to see everything clearly. It was Shalabh, who had come to pick me up to go to the function. A few dried pages crackled under his feet. The noise drew his attention to the forest of pages – his sophistication might have led him to call it a garden. He was baffled for a bit. Then he started looking over the room slowly, peering into the corners, as my words led his turning neck. Pages from the diary lay here, and on the other side of the room too. Scattered across the middle of the room were two scripts comprising around sixty to sixty-five pages. Every shelf in the cupboard housed more pages from the diary. Tiptoeing his way through them, he moved forward as I showed him the washroom. Some papers lay there as well. I showed him the pages that hung from the rope I had fashioned by tying my shirt and trousers together.

'These are Rafique's papers – his diary, his script. Look at his language.' I showed him a page that elaborately described the meeting with Amandeep. 'Just read the descriptions. He is a poet. This is the first time I have seen someone so candid even in a diary.'

'Who? He is a jihadi, boss!'

'No, there is no such Rafique, sir. What leaps out of these pages is his dedication, the struggles he has faced, and the work he is doing. I have no other word for him but "genius".'

His forehead erupted with furrows as he began to think. 'Why has he been targeting Hindu girls then?' he asked softly.

'Hello, mister, don't give me this official bullshit. There is some other war going on in your town, and I think all of you are involved. Anybody who loves this town would not stand to hear anything bad about such an amazing person. Are you aware – but how could you be? You should know that another student of Rafique has been made to disappear.

Tell your city's residents to cook up new stories, submit them as facts, start claiming that he is involved in a love triangle now.'

As I spoke, I got a lump in my throat. Perhaps because the last two days had exhausted me, or perhaps because of the helplessness I felt since I couldn't do anything for Anasuya, or perhaps because I had been overpowered by those who played this game. My voice first became hoarse, then it choked. There was something in this choking that made Shalabh leave the room. To overcome my tears, I went back to the pages. Reading them was like turning illusion into reality.

18/7/15

We've performed it twice as a street play, and people are beginning to like it. Performing on 15 August will be a great opportunity for others to watch it. If it can make even one person rise up against a murderous mob, our mission will be successful. It's the perfect moment to stage the play, but nobody is giving us the space for it. We had rented the Hindi Pracharini Sabha's hall for Independence Day. We had even paid Rs 3,400 for shows over two days. But then we were told it would not be possible since the hall was being repaired. How can we expect to rely on others when our own college has not given us the space to perform this play? People often refuse to look in the mirror because they fear the reflection may show a criminal's face.

9/7/15

Dadda had sent for us. All of us went over – Neeraj, Mukesh, Kushal, Aniruddha, Jagdish, Janaki and me. He wants us to perform Jaishankar Prasad's Chandragupt *at the Dol Mela this time. His university will arrange the funds and the venue for rehearsals. Dadda is polite but imposing at the same time, so even though it was difficult to say, I still asked him to watch a performance of* Bachane Wala Hai Bhagwan! *at least once. I told him if he just said the word, any place in the town would give us a stage. He said he was too busy to watch our play, but asked us to think about the other one. As the character named Amangal says – Let ... us ... see ... what ... happens...*

17/7/15

This road leads to Swami Devanand Degree College. The potholes to the side are brimming with black water. There is a culvert, and several passers-by. Niyaz lies down on the culvert with his head to the south and feet pointing north. Anuradha's touch alerts Niyaz to the fact that she has arrived. The evening itself is most pleased to see these two, so pleased that the sun refuses to set.

Niyaz: You've come?

Anuradha (taking a seat on the culvert): So it would seem.

[Silence for a couple of beats.]

Anuradha: My uncle is in the market today. He had called.

Niyaz: Say, we have to leave now.

Anuradha: Understand, we have to leave now.

Niyaz: Understood, we have to leave now.

Anuradha: Must you stand atop your pedestal and ridicule others all the time, Neju? Is this what your Allah-Allah-Khair-Salla has taught you?

Niyaz: He has also taught me that people should not be late, but they are.

Anuradha: Stop it.

Niyaz: Stopped it.

[A beat.]

Niyaz: Rakesh and Supriya went to the lodge.

Anuradha: Find someone else you can go to a lodge with.

Janaki's voice became sharp while delivering this line, the way it does when a body part emerges into the cold during harsh winter. She too had slipped out of Anuradha's character for a moment and become Janaki. Her face had started to burn. She needs to rehearse.

Oh god!

Amandeep was right, as was my suspicion. Anasuya's trust wasn't misplaced either. But a collective system had first rendered us isolated, and then imposed its story on our reality.

The programme was supposed to begin from 2 p.m. There was still some time left – long enough for me to clarify my position to the protectors of this town's image whom I'd met the night before last. My act of changing the setting of my Facebook post on their insistence, so that it was visible only to me, began to irk me. I changed the post's setting to public again, and during the time I should have spent reading Rafique's diary, I calmly put up another post with updates. I made sure it would not upset those who worried about the town's image either:

> *I am in Noma. The people here are nice and friendly. The entire town is busy with the preparations for the Dol Mela. The town has been trying to establish this festival as its unique identity for a few years now. Besides preparing for it, everyone is anxious that the festival should take place in a dignified manner. But a few destructive forces are also at work. My family friend Rafique, about whom I had said in my previous post that he had not returned home and had sought help, continues to be missing. One of his students, named Janaki, is also missing. The police, which until yesterday had refused to register an FIR, and the newspapers that could not find any space for the news, are brazenly*

calling it a matter of love jihad today. But nobody has any evidence to show for it. More tragically, Kushalpal, another one of Rafique's students, has not returned home since yesterday. It remains to be seen what story will now be put together about him.

After writing this, I thought for a while about whether to post it or not. There was no point in asking for someone's opinion, because they were all far away. In any case, if anything went wrong, it was on me. Second, if the town was so conscious about its image, then it should do good deeds. You cannot laugh and pout at the same time.

I pressed 'Post'.

Anybody would be amazed when they saw the campus of that deemed university. Spread over more than forty acres, it looked like the headquarters of some large corporation. The guards were probably familiar with Shalabh's jeep, so they let us in without any checks and without requiring us to sign anywhere. I had requested Sahadeo to follow me, and Shalabh had objected to it. For some reason, I hadn't liked his act of barging in and offering to drive me out here, so I didn't pay any heed to his objections.

A river called the Chhoti Gandak flowed on the northern and eastern ends of the campus. Pointing to it, Shalabh said it was the perfect place to set up a pharmaceutical plant. 'If the next government wishes, our state could turn into a pharma-manufacturing hub after the elections, just as Himachal Pradesh used to be once upon a time.'

Thinking I'd read whenever I'd get the time, I was carrying around fifty or sixty dried pages from Rafique's diary in my laptop bag. I was also carrying three sets of notes-like texts that had been made by stapling together four-five pages. But I got so carried away by the beauty of this campus that I couldn't find the time to do so.

The programme was to be held in the central auditorium, which was exquisitely decorated and equipped with state-of-the-art facilities. There were chairs on three sides of the stage. The hall, which looked like it could hold a thousand, was reasonably, if not fully, occupied. A closer look revealed they were mostly students. The university's dignitaries were seated in the first two rows. A long session of introductions followed. Barring the fact that Dadda was very cordial towards me, nothing else was memorable. After a while, when the conversations began to subside and only the voices from the stage could be heard, I saw that barely any of the young men I had met at the party were present. Perhaps they were busy with their work.

In all, twenty-three people were invited up to the stage. I grew worried at the thought that if everybody took even ten minutes to speak, the programme would last four hours. But no, this was not a government university where everyone held sway over their own little domains. There was only Dadda here.

The ambience reminded me of other functions so much that I became uneasy and got busy with my phone to distract myself. There were two messages:

'What date should I book the tickets for? Do answer your phone once in a while.'

'I won't be able to go to Delhi, Arjun. I am sending Jagdish's number.'

At first glance, it seemed that those who were on stage were people who loved functions and would go to any if invited. But I was proved wrong. Every speaker began

by extolling Dadda's virtues and ended with that day's
news – all of them gave a lecture on love jihad. Even
Ratnashankar, who used to insult Rafique all the time, was
there, and he stepped up and spat out numerous theories
about love jihad. When he introduced himself to me, I began
to abhor my own hand which he had shaken. I wanted to
tell him that I already knew about him. What was slightly
surprising was that all the speakers would have been
counted among the town's intellectuals, and yet everybody
thought the same as the newspaper report. Every speaker
underscored the crisis love jihad represented.

When it was my turn, the emcee, a young teacher at this
deemed university, insisted that I read out a story. And I
did. A whole story.

But...

But...

But I had not come here just to read a story. This town
had gobbled up a brilliant artist and a talented author. His
diary was the perfect illustration of this. It testified to his
heroism. But it didn't matter one bit to this town whether
he lived or not. Or maybe it did matter – which is why he
had been made to disappear.

Before commencing my reading, I paid back what I owed
from the other night. I began by saying:

'I won't mind if you don't listen to my story, but I request
your attention for what I am about to say now. Various
ludicrous accusations have been thrown around about
Rafique in the garb of legal language. But I remained quiet.
I remained quiet because he was not my friend. Yesterday,

a police official gently threatened me, saying that if people came to know I was his wife's ex-boyfriend, it could lead to a furore. Several among you will admit to being told that my reason for coming to your town is to see my ex. Think about it, someone like me, on the brink of middle age, has come to meet his ex! These fictions have been cobbled together to scare me. It might happen that tomorrow or day after or even later, you will get to read about me. So, I thought about telling you all up front.

'Anasuya is my friend, and her husband has gone missing, has vanished. Would you believe it? A man disappears in this small town and nobody knows anything! The police don't register a case. The daroga assures me that he will find Rafique, but eventually unearths a falsehood that it is a case of love jihad. Since Janaki, a student of that Rafique, has also gone missing.

'You will probably come to know in a day or two through these same dishonest newspapers that yet another student of Rafique has gone missing. Let me tell you right away that a young man named Kushalpal has not returned home since last evening. How does someone disappear in a small town like this? And why are only those connected to Rafique's acting group going missing?

'I have been told that my Facebook post is tarnishing the image of this town. Please think it over and tell me what is happening, and why. I am hurt, but I don't know whom to ask for help. The stories in the papers may claim to have evidence, but what I have is the trust garnered over the past three days by getting to know the lives of Rafique, Janaki and Kushalpal.'

By the time I had said all this, more than half the dignitaries in the first row had stepped outside. Almost everyone on the stage had made their way out too. Dadda remained seated, however. My reading went on for almost forty minutes. What was astonishing was that when Dadda's name was respectfully called for delivering the presidential address, all those who had gone outside during my reading came back.

Dadda, in his own style, said he could not take the matter of Rafique and Janaki seriously. He thanked me for telling them about the artists of their town despite being an outsider. I could have told him about his meetings with Rafique as well, which had been recorded in the diary, but I thought it better to remain silent. I listened to him quietly. In the end, turning to his students, he said we needed to seek inspiration from our society's heroes and their lives. As an inspirational example, however, he talked about Vajashrava – the sage who gave his son away to the god of death when the boy dared to correct his father's mistakes.

We sat in Dadda's office after the programme ended. Those who had been at the party the other night slowly began to arrive. There were several others as well. Dadda praised my statement and my story in front of everyone. 'Whatever be the thinking behind them, the stories you write are about love,' he added. I could only smile wanly.

Then I noticed I was getting a call. It was Amandeep. I stepped outside to receive it.

What Amandeep told me chilled me to the bone. Mukesh too had not returned home since morning. Amandeep also said someone from the police station had tipped him off that my phone might be tapped. 'Sir, listen to me and leave this town,' he said. Then he added hesitantly, 'If possible, take Jagdish and Niyaz with you.'

'And you? Will you stay here?'

He hung up without replying.

I could not respond to his suggestions over the phone, so I remained silent. When I went inside, I asked Dadda's permission to approach him. I requested him to arrange a meeting with his son, Amit Malviya. He agreed. 'He too wants to meet you. Would you like to come to his office, or should I send him over to your hotel?'

The news of Mukesh's disappearance rattled me. I remained speechless as I stepped out of Dadda's office and got into the car. I was stunned. I don't know what made me open Facebook, but when I did, I saw a notification that both my posts had been removed and I had been banned from posting anything for three days.

What on earth was going on in this settlement? I had no answers. All that seemed to be in my power was to demote Noma, which didn't seem to have any respect for the rule of law, from town to settlement. A settlement that was still a jungle. Whom could I ask for help? Without stopping to hear my own answer, I asked Sahadeo to halt the car. We were on a slope just after the bridge over the river Gandak which connected Mehrauna in Uttar Pradesh with Guthni in Bihar.

I called Archana as soon as I stepped out of the car and asked her, 'Do you know anyone who works for foreign media?'

'Why? What happened? Why aren't you coming back?'

'In the last three days, four people have gone missing or have been made to go missing.'

'Where are you?'

'Right here, in this country. I'm going mad.'

'Come back. Otherwise, I will inform Bhaiyya.'

'I have to evacuate five people. Talk to the human rights commission, please.' As soon as I said this, I couldn't help thinking that whoever was a member of the human rights commission in this town would also be one of *them*.

'What about you?'

'That would make it six. Jagdish, Amandeep, Anasuya, Niyaz, and me.'

'Who is the sixth one?'

'The one in Anasuya's womb.'

She went silent. I was quiet too. This was no time for words and understanding. Archana resumed, 'Ravi Bhaiyya will help in every possible way. But please, you get out of that town now!'

'These people have got my Facebook, Twitter, everything blocked.'

'Arjun, please, get to Gorakhpur. I will handle it from there.'

'No, if you can, please handle things from here to Gorakhpur. Ask your brother to call me.'

'But you leave that place right now.'

I was not going anywhere.

Getting into the car, I told Sahadeo: 'Suhag Studio.'

THE STATE OF THE ROAD was awful. This was not fully accurate, because while the left side of the road was riddled with potholes while returning to Noma from Mehrauna, the right side didn't seem to have any discernible problems barring a few spots. One reason for this could be that the heavy vehicles, the cargo-laden trucks that entered Uttar Pradesh from Bihar far outnumbered the ones going in the opposite direction. This must have been going on for a fairly long time; that's how roads crumble in such an asymmetrical manner.

I had to read while on that bumpy road. I took out the stapled papers this time, instead of the diary. There was a script among them. Another bunch had just three pages with the date 17 June 2015 written on top. This was the description of a meeting with Amandeep. The brittle paper kept disintegrating into tiny pieces in my hand, and it was difficult to read on that terrible road. This is what was written:

What was supposed to be a blazing-hot afternoon turned out to be one of unseasonal downpour. Jagdish and Mukesh were walking ahead. As soon as we felt

the first drops, they went to the shade of Adarsh PCO.
Kushalpal ran ahead as well, but he must have realized
that Janaki and I would be left behind, so he stopped.
We went inside a tea shop. The rain grew heavier. The
sky became dark. The two shops were not far from each
other, but the downpour made the distance between
them seem much greater. Kushal tried to say something
to Janaki. But the only sounds one could hear were of
the falling rain and the wind. The ten or twelve people
inside the tea shop were all gazing outside at the rain.
Not a single person spoke; perhaps they found it a
good time to get acquainted with themselves. Kushal
gestured: Tea? When he heard a 'yes' in response, he
turned to the tea shop owner and gestured: Two. Then
he brought his fingers close to say: Just a little bit. The
tea shop owner picked up the pot and pointed outside as
if to say: Strange. Both Janaki and Kushal mirrored his
gesture together: Yes, strange. All three of them laughed.

While sipping on her tea, Janaki attempted to lighten
the sombre mood and asked, 'Have you played the role
of a policeman before?' As Kushal began to respond,
he noticed a cut on her nose. 'What's this?' he asked.
Startled by his question, she shifted her glass to the other
hand and ran her fingers over the tip of her nose. 'This?'
She began to laugh. Kushal answered her first question
then. 'Yes. As a matter of fact, the company that I
perform road shows and street plays for receives several
scripts where a policeman commits atrocities.' He took

his card out of his pocket and handed it to Janaki. She gazed at it for a while, turning it over.

The skies cleared as soon as the rain stopped, as if daylight had broken out again. The spectacle – where everything appeared washed and cleansed, and the air turned light – entranced everyone. It was magical, except for the smell. Rainwater had permeated all living and non-living things in such a way that the downpour brought out whatever smell resided within them. The soil, the shops, the streets, the men, the dogs – it seemed as if each had a unique smell that imbued the air with its earthiness. Janaki could discern every smell with accuracy. She saw both Jagdish and Mukesh coming to them. Jagdish apologized as soon as he entered. Everyone laughed. He was embarrassed about abandoning his new guests at such a difficult time. Then he realized that the rain perhaps didn't count as a difficult time. Janaki began to talk about the pervasive smell. She wanted to describe the many scents in the same detail in which they had pervaded her mind. Everyone listened, but Janaki soon realized that she needn't describe it in such detail, sensing that the others were getting used to and also identifying the smells themselves.

It was five in the evening by the time we reached Amandeep's house. Jagdish had met him before. Just like the last time, he saw that Aman's father answered the door. He was an elderly man. Jagdish touched his feet. As soon as he bent down, the rest of us looked at each other, as if we had gone off-script. Regardless, we took turns to touch his feet. Jagdish's first question was supposed to be related to his health. Instead, he asked, 'Is Aman Sahib home?' They heard Aman's voice, 'Come up.' He was looking down from the balcony, his hair untied. When everyone was inside his room, Aman asked formally, 'Any trouble coming here?' He glanced outside the window then closed it. His question was really not as formal as Jagdish's laughter made it sound. The windowpane was broken. Taking a seat, Aman said his house had once again been pelted with stones two nights ago.

Mukesh, who had not even sat down properly, sprang up. 'Pelted with stones? But you're a policeman, Sardar-ji!' Everyone stayed quiet. Mukesh sat back on the beanbag. Kushal flipped through the script and asked Jagdish: 'Is this stone-pelting part of the script? I guess not?' Jagdish shook his head to say no. 'You've read it already?'

The room was dimly lit. The fan had been switched on, and a calendar printed in the Gurmukhi script fluttered in its breeze. Some pictures had been put up on the wall, not as much for decoration as to fill the void in the room. There were three pictures of his family. One of them featured his wife and two daughters. He said that he had sent them over to his village in Bareilly district. In another photo, his wife was seated as he stood touching her shoulder. The third had several people in it. All three were put up on a wall together.

The remaining pictures were all related to his job. Seven of them were newspaper clippings that had been framed. They carried news of Amandeep's bravery or awards he had won. At the very top was an article titled 'Babhnan Robbery Case Unravelled: Mastermind Killed in Encounter'. The strap read, 'Young inspector Amandeep's bravery praised by DGP'. The clipping carried two faded images that had almost disappeared with time. One of them was a passport-sized photo of a smiling Amandeep, and the other had a police jeep and a dead man lying next to it. Peering over at them, Mukesh asked, 'How many years have you been in the police?'

'Twelve or thirteen.' As he spoke, he looked over at me and couldn't help blurting out, 'Is he going to play Niyaz? If he sports a thin moustache, no one will be able to tell the difference between him and the real Niyaz.' Then he turned to Jagdish. 'Were you able to meet him?'

Jagdish told Aman they were only able to meet Niyaz on the third attempt, and that too, when they had gone to his place accompanied by Naseem Siddiqui, a mathematics teacher from O.K. Inter College. They had spoken to him for a fair bit.

Jagdish stood up as he filled Aman in, then introduced his new companions while walking up to their chairs. It was all very awkward, but he had to start somewhere. Grabbing Kushal by the shoulders, he exclaimed, 'It is all thanks to this man. Kushalpal Singh – he is playing you.'

The two eyed each other as if looking into a mirror. Adulation and deference were apparent in Kushal's eyes. Amandeep seemed to be looking at the future. He said, 'Mind you, it's suspended assistant sub-inspector Amandeep. And please don't call this a project my friend. It was a matter of life and death for us. I mean, for Niyaz, Anuradha and me.' He laughed and added, 'Whenever someone praises me, I feel like I am sitting at my own funeral.'

Everyone laughed. As Jagdish introduced Janaki, the first word he uttered was, 'Anuradha.'

'And this is Rafique Sir. He will play Niyaz.'

Then Amandeep asked, 'And who will play the part of the criminal Amit Malviya and his goons? It's not easy to find scoundrels of that calibre.' The disgust in his voice was palpable.

Silence reigned over the room for a few moments. The calendar too stopped fluttering and went quiet. The other four looked at me. The silence would have continued had Jagdish not spoken up. 'I, Jagdish Upadhyay, will play him,' he dramatically declared to lighten the mood again. Amandeep bit his tongue. He was a daroga after all, even if he was suspended – he probably couldn't remember the last time he had said sorry to anyone. He touched his ears in apology. As if this was not enough, he went up to Jagdish and embraced him. Jagdish, trapped in this bear hug, finally realized how big Amandeep was.

Amandeep apologized again, 'Bhai, I was not calling you a scoundrel.'

'Of course. You were cursing Amit. Why would I mind that?' Jagdish said.

'I thought since you were playing his part, you might take it otherwise.'

What Aman said surprised all four of them. Nobody said a word, but they were all forced to contemplate the assumptions people make about acting.

Aman tried to steer the conversation in a different direction. 'Will you be able to play the role of such a cunning and insidious man?' Jagdish could only respond with a deep sigh.

The subject had to be changed. Jagdish asked Aman, 'Mukesh wants to know – how did you find the courage to take on a crowd?'

Amandeep laughed heartily. There were many layers to his laughter, but right at the top was his age. He must have been around thirty-five. He said, 'I often ask myself how I did that. And now...' – he was perhaps alluding to his suspension – '... I wonder why I did so. Why on earth did I do that? If I had known that this was a deliberate plan for murder, I might not have saved him.'

Jagdish: Yes, but you saved a person's life.

Aman: And lost my job.

Mukesh: Are you certain you've been suspended because you saved Niyaz?

Aman: Oh, damn this certainty! Listen, you guys should know better than to get into trouble needlessly. What we had believed – or at least I had – to be an ordinary incident is nothing but a parallel system coming to life. These people are from an entirely different world. Instead of the police, they have their own goons. Proper criminals. Earlier, this system used the police for all its murders, but now the police play second fiddle to them.

Janaki: But what a beautiful thing that this could actually happen – that the police reach on time and manage to save someone's life, whatever sort of life it may be. Such a tale needs to be told – like a prayer, like a lesson – to everyone!

Aman: I thought the same, until I received my letter of suspension. Let me show you the letter. What I have heard is that Dadda's son, Amit Malviya, and his scoundrels were reprimanded at the state-level meeting of the Morcha. They couldn't kill even a single vidharmi, a single heretic, and yet they thought Dadda deserved to be given a ticket for the state and central elections? These people got me suspended after that meeting. They are sending a message to the police.

When Aman opened his cupboard, Mukesh saw his uniform neatly hanging from a rod, the shirt and trousers on separate hangers. A neatly tied turban lay on the top shelf. Aman showed us his suspension letter, warning us that we should think twice before doing a street play on the incident. Mukesh was the closest, so he saw the letter first. Aman explained that he had been suspended on the charge that he had been misappropriating funds for eight years.

Kushal: Was there any misappropriation?

Aman: I don't remember.

It was difficult to get there in the evening. The narrow street leading to Swami Devanand Degree College from Noma's market was dotted with several other photo studios. This street too passed through the vegetable market. Sahadeo parked close to the trucks that must have brought vegetables in the morning. He took a good look around as he parked and locked the car. Only when he was satisfied did he hurriedly walk across to me. I had told him earlier that I was afraid of being left alone.

There it was, Suhag Studio! True to its name, the entrance stood between grimy windows where several wedding photos were on display. Most of them had been digitally enhanced. Inside, the light was bright and the counter small. Behind it sat an elderly man. Seeing us come in, he pointed towards some seating and asked us to wait for a bit. He must have thought we had come to get our photos taken.

Gathering my courage, I said, 'Sir, we are here to see Niyaz.'

He froze, like a statue. Then he shook his head. Only after we explained the whole situation did the fear vanish from his face. He went to the back of the shop. As he started climbing the stairs, we noticed there was a section upstairs. This was his home too. Before he could come down, three people emerged from the back room, which was the studio. A woman accompanied by a man, both clearly here to get their picture taken. A tall and well-built middle-aged man walked behind them. He prepared their invoice, and taking half the amount as advance, asked them to return in two days.

Then he turned to us. Before I could speak, Sahadeo took over.

The time this was taking was beginning to annoy me. I glanced at my phone and saw two missed calls and two messages. All from Archana:

'Arjun, avoid any kind of trouble until tomorrow, please. Just until tomorrow.'

'Bhaiyya has spoken to the Human Rights Commission. They may come with us tomorrow.'

Under normal circumstances, I would have dwelt more on the question: When was the last time I had seen Archana this impatient?

Climbing down the almost-dark stairs, the elderly man gestured for us to come up.

It was extremely narrow upstairs. There were two rooms, either nine-by-ten or ten-by-ten feet. We were asked to sit in the first room. A little while later, the elderly man came out of the second room with three others. By now, I had understood who he was. He introduced the others. The elderly lady was Niyaz's mother, there was Niyaz's sister Mehrunnisa, and Niyaz himself.

After the initial exchange of pleasantries, I asked to speak with Niyaz privately. His mother blessed the policeman who had saved her son's life as she left.

Once Niyaz was alone, I said, 'Amandeep insisted we meet you.'

Niyaz said that Amandeep had called him too. He had implored Niyaz to leave town with the help of the person who was going to visit him.

'But how did this happen? And why? And wasn't there a girl with you as well, Anuradha? Where is she now?'

'I haven't understood it myself, even until today. There were two other boys with me in that group, both my classmates in BSc final year. But all they wanted was a Muslim. They would have killed me if I was alone.'

'How were your results?' I quipped to lighten the mood.

'What results, sir? I was determined to take the exams, but Ammi put her foot down. My brother too sided with her. I'm not sure whether I can enrol this year.'

What could be said after such an answer?

Niyaz himself resumed the conversation. 'I am afraid to go to college.'

'Will you come to Delhi?'

He didn't say anything.

'You may have heard that those associated with the theatre group are going missing.'

'Yes, I read in today's paper. Our fear has multiplied many times over.' His response put to rest all my disjointed questions.

'It's all fake news,' I said. 'This is no case of love jihad. There's nothing going on between Rafique and Janaki. Other people from the group have also disappeared.'

'I don't know what is real and what is fake, but they were good people. Once they found out where I lived, they visited me thrice. Every time they asked me to play myself in their production. I refused. I didn't know whether I could act or not. And I was terrified. I didn't object to the use of my name. Niyaz could be anybody. And every time I saw Rafique playing me, I thought he was a better Niyaz than I was. He took me along to all of their performances. It felt as if he had internalized how I spoke, how I walked, how I looked at things – and everything else. When I was attacked, I didn't feel the fear of death at that moment as much as during the times I saw Rafique Sir acting out that scene. I cried every time. I watched the play thrice, and every time I thought Rafique Sir would be killed for real if the policemen in the play didn't arrive on time.'

'But weren't there four performances?'

'Yes, the last performance was on 15 August. But they could not finish it.'

'Why?'

'The theatre group performed at the college grounds on the afternoon of Independence Day. They had made me a part of their team. Every performance attracted a bigger crowd than the previous one. There was a sizeable crowd that day too. I liked how they thought that if they publicized the instances when people saved the lives of others, people would then stop playing with others' lives, or if needed, would even save them. But the actors were attacked before the performance could finish. The assault took place despite the presence of the police.'

'Then?'

'When I saw people from the Morcha among the attackers, I was sure they were the same people who wanted to kill me. It would have been a blood-soaked 15 August had there not been an audience. When others stepped forward to mediate, the attackers left the scene. But before leaving, they announced on the mike that they would not allow the play to be performed in this town again.'

Even if Niyaz had not told me this last bit, things were becoming crystal clear. Niyaz was connecting the threads with his memory. It must have been terrifying for him just to recount all of this.

'I remember the look on Amit's face as he hit me. There was a look of calm, rather than one of fury. Amandeep Sahib was sent by Allah to save me. Nobody would have even found my corpse had he not been there. But Amit had already attacked twice with an iron rod before he arrived.' He lifted his shirt. The skin around his right shoulder was peeled off.

After he showed us the wound, Niyaz set his shirt back in place with great discomfort. Conscious of his pain, I said, 'The other wound must be similar, I imagine. Or is it worse?'

A strange smile appeared on his face. 'No, you cannot imagine.'

'Sorry, I didn't mean to say I don't want to see your wounds. You looked uncomfortable, that's why I said you didn't have to show it.'

'Exactly – that's why I said you cannot imagine. Before Amit could hit me a second time, Anuradha came between us and shielded me, the way a roof protects a house. She didn't even get the chance to cry out in pain. If I had taken that blow, I wouldn't have been able to cry out either. The attackers backed off when they saw what had happened. That's when Amandeep Sahib was able to save me.

'You had asked about that girl. Sir, Anuradha's life is hanging by a thread at a hospital in Mumbai.'

We stayed silent for a long time. Before leaving, I asked Niyaz if he would testify in case the matter ever went to court.

He couldn't answer. Not because he didn't want to, but because his mother loudly asked me to leave as soon as she heard the word 'court'.

The elderly man put his hands together in a namaste and saw us off with an expressionless face as we walked out of the shop.

Night had fallen. Several lights were being installed along the street as decorations for the festival. There were ladders, people, the market. The Dol Mela was two days away. That's why the streets were jammed.

Shalabh called several times, but I didn't answer. To tell the truth, my mind was blank. The darkness behind all the light did not let me think. A couplet by the last Mughal king Bahadur Shah Zafar kept coming back to me over and over again: '*Main sisakta reh gaya aur mar gaye Farhad-o-Qais.*' All I could do was weep, but Farhad and Qais gave up their lives … If civilization has indeed progressed, it should have progressed in a direction where no one needed to see their beloved killed in front of them or made to disappear. But we hadn't been able to do so in all these years. What could I have told Anasuya? That we would be able to find Rafique as well as clear the web of lies that had been spun around his life? His diary, his notes, his script – all of them were telling the truth, but what was available to everyone was the newspapers, the police, the Morcha, and their homicidal ambitions.

Somewhere among the papers stuffed in my bag and the ones scattered all over my room was the script of this entire play. If I could sleep, I wanted to dream about Rafique and his companions performing the play during the Dol Mela. Then, a moment would come where I would find it difficult to tell whether the person playing Niyaz was Rafique, or whether it was someone like me who had entered Rafique's being to play Niyaz.

24/8/15

The Dol Mela is on 5 September. It is also our test. Looking at the circumstances, each of us will have to rehearse the roles of all the characters from today onwards. This will ensure that the performance can go on even if, god forbid, only one person is left. How I wish seven or eight of us could play all the characters by ourselves, so that we could perform the play in seven or eight different places at once.

If there comes a time to perform this play all by yourself, then know that it should be executed like a street performer's show. One prop for each character, for easy identification. A police hat for Amandeep. For Mangal, his scarf. A weapon for Amangal. For Niyaz, his books. Remember, he is a student of science. An intelligent student. Keep two flowers for Anuradha. One to adorn herself with and the other for...

I found out today that the drum used by street performers costs 400 rupees. We will get it. We will buy it beforehand, because it needs to be tightened for a good sound, and we will have to learn to pull its strings to tune it.

We will have to start with the drum and there is no harm in this.

But we will have to come up with catchy lines to go along with the beat.

And lastly, which means right before starting the performance, you must ask the spectators to sit down. The stage is your home. Explain to the audience the story you are going to tell them. It's not going to be easy to convince them that the one who saves is god.

This novel is dedicated to the brave Uttarakhand police officer, Gagandeep Singh, who saved a young man from a lynch mob.